Poppy's Return

Read all the adventures of Poppy and friends

RAGWEED ★ POPPY ★ POPPY AND RYE
ERETH'S BIRTHDAY ★ POPPY'S RETURN

And enjoy these books by Avi

The Barn

Beyond the Western Sea, Book I: The Escape from Home

Beyond the Western Sea, Book II: Lord Kirkle's Money

Blue Heron

Devil's Race

Don't You Know There's a War On?

Encounter at Easton

The Fighting Ground

Finding Providence

The Man Who Was Poe

The Mayor of Central Park

Never Mind! with Rachel Vail

Night Journeys

Nothing but the Truth

Prairie School

Romeo and Juliet—Together (and Alive!) at Last

Smugglers' Island

Something Upstairs

Sometimes I Think I Hear My Name

S.O.R. Losers

The True Confessions of Charlotte Doyle

"Who Was That Masked Man, Anyway?"

Windcatcher

~ AVI ~

Poppy's Return

ILLUSTRATED BY *Brian Floca*

HarperCollins*Publishers*

Fx: 09105

Poppy's Return

Text copyright © 2005 by Avi

Illustrations copyright © 2005 by Brian Floca

The illustrations are drawn with

Eberhard Faber Design Ebony pencils on Stonehenge paper.

www.harperchildrens.com

Library of Congress Cataloging-in-Publication Data

Avi, 1937-

Poppy's return / by Avi ; illustrated by Brian Floca.— 1st ed.

p. cm.

Summary: Poppy, accompanied by her troublesome son Junior, his
skunk friend, and Uncle Ereth the porcupine, responds to a summons
to return to her ancestral home, Gray House, to save the mice there
from destruction by a bulldozer.

ISBN 0-06-000012-0 — ISBN 0-06-000013-9 (lib. bdg.)

[1. Family problems—Fiction. 2. Prejudices—Fiction. 3. Mothers and
sons—Fiction. 4. Mice—Fiction. 5. Skunks—Fiction. 6. Porcupines—
Fiction.] I. Floca, Brian, ill. II. Title.

PZ7.A928Pop 2005   2004030054

[Fic]—dc22   CIP

                                                                AC

Typography by Karin Paprocki

1 2 3 4 5 6 7 8 9 10

❖

First Edition

For *my* family

Contents

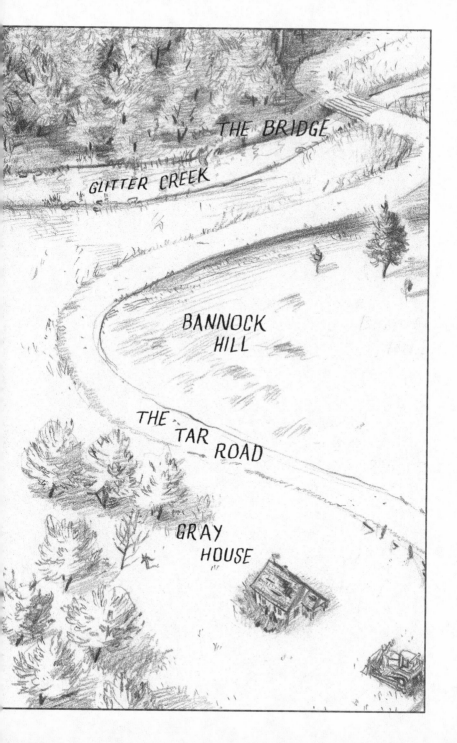

Poppy's Return

CHAPTER I

Poppy and Rye Visit Ereth

S UGARED SLUG SOUP," said Ereth the porcupine without looking up from the lump of salt over which he was slobbering. "I don't believe it."

"I'm afraid it's true," said the deer mouse Poppy to her old friend. "It's very upsetting. The kind of thing that makes me wonder if I've been a bad parent."

Poppy and her husband, Rye, a golden mouse, had gone over to Ereth's smelly hollow log for a talk. The closest of friends, they lived deep within Dimwood Forest, where the tall trees reached into the sweet air and carpeted the earth below with soft shadows.

"Now Poppy," said Rye, "the rest of our children are doing fine."

Poppy sighed. "I suppose one failure out of a litter of eleven isn't bad," she said. Her round, white belly had

grown plump of late. Though her eyes were usually bright
and her whiskers full, now those eyes appeared rather dull
and full of worry, while her whiskers were somewhat limp.

"You made your first mistake by naming him Ragweed
Junior," Ereth grumbled between licks of salt. "Most *jun-
iors*," he said, "resent the name. Or should."

"I wish he *did* resent it," said Poppy. "Junior's problem
is that he *loves* being a new Ragweed."

"Gangrenous gym shorts," said Ereth. "Was there ever
a mouse—dead or alive—who caused more fuss than the
first Ragweed?"

"I'm afraid," said Rye, "Junior wants to be what he *thinks* Ragweed was. It's all those stories he's heard about my brother."

"Though of course," Poppy said, "Junior never knew Ragweed. All he knows is that Ragweed was unusual." She reached out, took Rye's paw, and squeezed it with affection. "It was Ragweed who brought us together. And if it hadn't been for him," she reminded Ereth, "I doubt you and I would have met."

"I suppose," said Ereth. He put his salt lump down reluctantly. "Just what the flea fudge has Junior done?"

"He used to be a cheerful, chatty, wonderfully open young mouse," said Poppy. "Nowadays it's a constant frown."

"If I say yes," Rye went on, pulling at his long whiskers, "he says no. If I say no, he says yes. When he says anything more than that, it's mostly 'Leave me alone.'"

"He has become rather rude," said Poppy.

"Almost impossible to get him out of bed before noon," added Rye.

"I doubt," said Poppy, "that he washes his face more than once a week, even though he's constantly being reminded." Her own ears were large and dark, with a nose, toes, and tail that were pink and clean.

"And now he's completely changed his looks," said Rye,

whose fur was dark orange.

"*Looks!*" barked Ereth. "How can a mouse change his looks?"

"You see," said Rye, with a shake of his head and a whisk of his tail, "Junior's best friend is a skunk."

The salt fell from Ereth's paws. "A *skunk?*"

"His name is Mephitis," Poppy explained. "We don't know much about him. Or his family. I'm afraid the problem is that he's not a very good influence. Ereth, you need to see Junior for yourself."

"Oh, toe jam on a toothpick," said Ereth. "He can't be that bad."

"The point is," said Poppy, "Junior has become a teenager."

"A teenager!" cried the porcupine. "Why the weasel wonk did you let that happen?"

"He did it on his own," said Rye, his small ears cocked forward.

"Then I'd better go unbuckle his buttons," said Ereth. With a rattle of his quills, he heaved himself up. "Where is he?"

"Probably down among the snag roots," said Rye. "He's taken to liking darkness, too."

"Just watch me, putt pockets," said Ereth. "I'll straighten him out flatter than a six-lane highway rolling through

Death Valley. Be back soon. But don't touch that salt, or you'll get a quill up your snoot." Quills rattling, the porcupine clumped out of the old log and headed for the gray lifeless and topless tree in which Poppy and her family made their home.

"Good luck," Rye called after him.

"I do hope it was all right to tell Ereth about Junior," said Poppy.

"Nothing else has worked," said Rye.

"But . . . what do you think he'll do?"

"I'm not sure, but I guess we'll find out pretty soon."

CHAPTER 2

Ragweed Junior

Serves poppy and rye right for having children," said Ereth as he waddled along the well-worn path that stretched between his log and the snag. Not the sweetest smelling of creatures, the old porcupine had a flat face with a blunt, black nose and fierce, grizzled whiskers. Sharp quills covered him from head to twitchy tail.

"They were much too young to have kids," he muttered. "No experience. Don't have enough strict rules. No consistency. No firmness. They spoil those youngsters. Let them run everything. Coddle them. I mean—baboon bubble bath—who's supposed to be in charge? Kids or parents? Well, it's time I taught them all a lesson or two about how a parent *should* act."

"Hi, Uncle Ereth. Where are you going?"

Ereth looked up. Some of Poppy and Rye's children were playing just outside the snag. Snowberry was building something out of sticks. Sassafras and Walnut were in deep conversation. It was Columbine who had called to him.

"Where's your brother?" Ereth demanded.

"I have a lot of brothers," said Columbine.

"The one who's acting like an idiot."

"Most of my brothers act like idiots," said Columbine with a cheerful grin.

"Listen here, you piddling pile of potted pips, don't talk back to me!"

The other mice looked around at one another. They loved to hear Ereth swear.

Columbine, barely managing not to giggle, said, "Which brother are you looking for?"

"Ragweed," said Ereth. "The junior variety."

"Oh, him," said Columbine, her good cheer fading. "What do you want *him* for?"

"I need to straighten him out."

"Uncle Ereth, if you want old grumpy, he's either with his friend Mephitis or down in the snag roots."

"I don't *want* him," said Ereth. "I don't *want* any of you. I need to *talk* to him."

The porcupine went to the base of the snag. Since the mouse entry hole was too small for him to pass through, the best he could do was stick in his snout and call: "Junior! This is your Uncle Ereth. I need to speak to you. Now!"

The young mice put aside what they were doing to

watch what would happen.

No reply came from inside the tree.

"Junior!" bellowed Ereth. "You get your bloated bean-bag of a brain up here or I'll unzip your bottom from your belly and give it the boot!"

The young mice waited breathlessly for a reply.

When none came, Ereth screamed, "Didn't you hear me? I said *now*!"

"I'm busy," said an irritated voice.

"With what?" said Ereth.

"Stuff."

"March yourself up here this moment," cried Ereth, "before I stuff your stuff up your stuffing!"

"Okay, okay. Keep your pit in your olive."

Ereth snarled and looked around at the mice. "What are you watching?" he cried.

"You," said Snowberry, no longer able to keep from giggling.

"Good. Maybe you'll learn something." His prickly tail thrashed back and forth, stirring up a large cloud of dust.

All eyes were on the entry hole. After what seemed forever, a mouse crawled out. Ereth blinked. Ragweed Junior had dyed his normally golden fur tar black. A white streak ran down his back. He looked like a miniature skunk.

"Yo, dude, what's going down?" said Junior.

"Is that you?" said Ereth. "Ragweed Junior?"

"Yeah. What do you want?"

"Why are you . . . that way?"

"What way?"

"Looking like a skunk, sounding like a frog."

"Because I freaking well want to."

"Bug-bellied bromides," said Ereth. "Don't swear at me like that. I'm your uncle."

"Yeah, well, if a porcupine can be an uncle to a mouse,

I can be a skunk," said Junior. "And if all you're going to do is yell at me, I've got better things to do." He turned to go.

"Hold it right there, young mouse!" yelled Ereth. "I'm here to tell you that this rudeness has to stop. You need to show some respect for your parents—the ones that raised you up, take care of you, and make sure your life is decent. Have you no gratitude?"

"Gratitude is for old grumps and gimps," returned Junior. "Listen, flat face, why don't you pick on someone your own size? Or better yet, to talk the way you do: go pack up your prickles and peddle some pickles for some pocket change!" With that, Junior spun about and disappeared back into the snag.

Ereth—his mouth agape—stared at the entry hole. "Bottled baby barf!" he cried. "He *has* become a teenager." The old porcupine hurried back toward his log.

The young mice, laughing uproariously, watched him go. "Did we learn anything?" said Snowberry.

It was Walnut who said, "Well, Junior is still grumpy."

To which Columbine added, "And Uncle Ereth is still funny."

CHAPTER 3

The Message

As ERETH HURRIED BACK to his log, he saw a mouse on the path. At first he thought she was Poppy. But when he realized she was a mouse he had never seen before, he skidded to a halt and stuck his nose close to her. "Who the musky muskrat marbles are *you*?"

"How do you do?" said the mouse, backing away nervously. "Are you Erethizon Dorsatum?"

"What if I was?"

"Might you be Poppy's . . . acquaintance?"

"I'm her best friend."

"How do you do, Mr. Dorsatum. My name is Lilly. I'm one of Poppy's siblings."

"You're . . . *what* kind of dribbling sap?"

"I am Poppy's sister."

"*Sister!* What sister? Where did you come from?"

"From Gray House," said Lilly. "That's Poppy's home on the south side of the forest. Beyond Glitter Creek.

Near Tar Road. Do you know where I might find Poppy? I'm bringing her an important message."

"I always know where she is," said Ereth. "Follow me."

"Thank you, Mr. Dorsatum," said Lilly. "I was apprehensive about getting to her in time."

"In time for what?"

"The news I'm bringing."

"Which is?"

"I'm sorry, Mr. Dorsatum. It's a . . . family matter."

"Oh, clown cheese! Just come with me." The porcupine marched to the entrance of his hollow log. "She's in here," he said to the mouse.

Lilly, who had been following behind Ereth, halted before the foul stench that wafted from the log. Looking about, she saw that the log's ancient bark was rust colored, encrusted by fungus that looked like limp angel wings. In the rotting soil that lay around the log grew damp and decaying mushrooms.

Lilly wrinkled her nose. "Here?" she said. "Does Poppy truly live here?"

"What's the matter with it?"

"It . . . has an . . . offensive odor."

"Cockroach-flavored chewing gum!" cried Ereth. "This happens to be *my* home, and it's where Poppy is visiting. You can come in or wait here. Suit yourself, lice wit, or whatever your name is." With a snort, Ereth went into the log, leaving Lilly behind.

Poppy and Rye were waiting for him. Instead of saying anything, Ereth marched to his salt lump and began to lick it, salivating loudly.

Poppy and Rye exchanged looks. Rye nodded, and Poppy went over to the porcupine. "Ereth, did you see Junior?"

"Yes."

"What did you think?"

"Not much."

"Did the two of you talk?"

"Humph."

"Ereth . . . please tell me what was said."

"I told him he was an idiot."

"Oh. And he said?"

"Called me flat face. Told me to pack up my prickles and go."

"I'm sorry," said Poppy, trying not to smile. "I'm afraid that's the way he is to everyone lately."

"Ereth," said Rye, "do you have any idea what we might do with him?"

"Get rid of him. Disown him. Drop him. Shoo him away. Give him the boot. Evict him. Exile him. Forget him. Tell him he's on his own. That he's not worth your trouble. That he's nothing but mildewed marmalade."

"Ereth," cried Poppy. "Those are awful things to say

about anyone, but Junior is our child. We can't do that to him. I . . . don't even want to. We love him."

"*Love,*" sneered Ereth. "Love is 'evil' spelled backward—with an *i* instead of an *o*."

"But he *needs* us," said Rye.

"The only one who needs you right now," muttered Ereth to Poppy, "is your sister."

"My sister?" exclaimed Poppy. "What in the world are you talking about?"

"The one who calls herself Little Bit and talks like she ate a book of manners. She's right outside. Waiting for you."

"She *is?*"

"Oh, peppered peacock pasta! Didn't I just say that?"

"Ereth," cried Poppy into his face, "sometimes you are impossible!" With that, she scampered around Ereth and out of the log, with Rye close at her heels.

"Mice," muttered Ereth to himself as he returned to his salt. "It would be more fun listening to glowworms grow!"

The moment Poppy emerged from the log, she saw her sister. "Lilly!" she cried, and threw her paws around her, covering Lilly's face with squeaky nuzzles. "But what are you doing here? How is everybody? When did you arrive? You look wonderful. What made you come? Oh, Lilly, this is my husband, Rye. Rye, this is Lilly. The oldest of my thirty-two little sisters." And she gave her

sister a new round of hugs and nuzzles.

"Pleasure to meet you," said Rye, grinning shyly and extending a paw to his sister-in-law.

"Very much obliged," said Lilly, offering a limp paw in return.

"You must meet our children," Poppy went on. "Or have you met them already? Some of them are right over there. There are eleven. All wonderful. You'll love them. They'll love you. Just come along. I am *so* glad to see you. How's Mama? How's Papa?"

"Poppy," said Lilly, "I'm afraid you're not giving me any time to reply."

"I'm sorry," said a laughing Poppy. "I'm so excited to see you."

"Poppy," said Lilly with great gravity, "it was Papa who dispatched me here."

The smile left Poppy's face. "Lilly, is something wrong?"

"Things are *not* good at home. Mama would like to see you, of course. But it's Papa: he's not well. He ordered me to bring you back as soon as possible. You see, there's a gigantic bulldozer parked right near Gray House. It appears as if humans plan to knock our house down. So, as far as the family is concerned, things could not be worse."

CHAPTER 4

A Decision

Poppy GATHERED TEN of the children and stood them before the entryway to the snag. At the same time Rye went down among the roots and insisted that Junior come out, too. When all had been assembled, Poppy introduced them to her sister. "Children, this is your Aunt Lilly. Aunt Lilly, this is Mariposa, Columbine, Verbena, Scrub Oak, Pipsissewa, Crabgrass, Locust, Sassafras, Walnut, Snowberry, and Ragweed Junior."

The young mice stared at the newcomer with intense curiosity.

"What do you say, children?"

"Pleased to meet you, Aunt Lilly," they chorused, except for Junior, who chose to stare glumly at the ground.

"And while we're very happy that Lilly came to visit," Poppy continued, "I'm afraid she's brought us sad news."

Poppy's tone made Junior look up. "It's about my father," she said. "Your grandfather, whom you've never met. Of course, I've talked about him. Remember? His name is Lungwort. Lilly has come to tell us he's not very well."

Lilly spoke up. "Your mother's papa—Lungwort—who is my father, too—asked me to come here. He very much needs your mother to visit."

"Can we come?" piped up Pipsissewa immediately.

Poppy and Rye exchanged looks. "That's something

we haven't decided," said Rye.

"But we will soon," said Poppy. "Because if I go, I'll need to leave quickly. Now why don't you show your aunt about while your father and I talk things over."

The young mice—all but Junior—gathered around Lilly and led her into the snag.

"Junior," said Rye, "aren't you going along with the others?"

"I'm going over to Mephitis's place."

Poppy tried not to show her disappointment. "Are his parents there?"

"Quit checking up on me all the time," said Junior. "I'm almost three months old. Not exactly a baby. I can take care of myself."

"Junior," said Rye, "it's the responsibility of parents to know where their children are at all times."

"Hey, Pops, aren't you forgetting?" said Junior. "When your brother Ragweed was four months old, he took off from home. Right? Right. Permanently. And what did you tell me Ragweed was always saying? 'A mouse has to do what a mouse has to do.' Did I get that right? So I figure I can pretty well take care of myself, too. That okay with you?" He started off.

"When will you be back?" Poppy called after him.

"Later," said Junior as he disappeared from view.

"Not very sympathetic, is he?" said Rye as he looked after his departing son.

"Rye," said Poppy, "Junior doesn't like us anymore."

"Hopefully it's just his age," said Rye. "And he'll get over it."

"But what if he doesn't?" said Poppy. "Oh my, it's hard when your own child turns against you."

"Let's talk about that later," said Rye, giving Poppy a nuzzle. "You need to decide what you're going to do."

"I don't think I have much choice," said Poppy. "They seem to need me to make a visit back there. Rye, it's been a long time since I've seen them. It will seem very strange. Why, none of them has ever met you, or the children."

"You never wanted us to."

"It was all so complicated."

"Do you think we should go?" said Rye.

"I'd love it if everyone could meet my family," said Poppy. "But it's a long trip. And you know the forest can be dangerous. It has many creatures—not all pleasant. No, there's no telling who's out there. And with so many straggling children in tow . . ."

"Then it's best we don't go," said Rye. "You'll travel faster that way. Both ways. But I will need to stay home," he pointed out. "Don't take offense, but the thought of you traveling alone . . ." He gave her a nuzzle.

"I've done it before," Poppy reminded him. She smiled at him. "Maybe I'm a little wiser now. And if Lilly can do it, surely so can I."

"I know, but . . ."

"No, I understand," said Poppy, taking up Rye's paw. "I'd feel the same if *you* were going off. And of course Lilly will be with me."

"Not on the way back."

"That's true." Poppy became thoughtful, and stared into the woods in the direction Junior had taken.

"Rye . . . ," she said, uncertainty in her voice. "Rye, what would you think if I took . . . Junior?"

"Good gracious! Why would you even want to?"

"Rye, I think I've lost contact with him—as a parent, 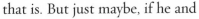 that is. But just maybe, if he and I traveled—just the two of us—it might bring us together. You know, something of an adventure. The worst that could happen is that it would go badly. Things could hardly be poorer than they are now. If we could get along, it might be something special.

Junior was right: Ragweed left home when he was four months old. This may be the last chance I'll have to be with Junior. Of course," she added, "I'll have to ask him if he wants to come."

"He might say no," Rye warned.

"I'm going to chance it," said Poppy.

"I do admire you, Poppy," said Rye with a grin. "But then," he added, "I always have."

"Thank you. And if Junior and I become friends again, the trip will be worth it."

When Aunt Lilly returned with the children, Poppy took her aside and informed her she would make the trip to Gray House. They could leave the next day.

"Oh, Poppy," said Lilly, "Papa will be gratified. So will Mama. You'll see, you will get on so much better with them than you used to. Papa's mellowed."

Poppy, however, said nothing about Junior coming. She wanted to speak to him first. And she dreaded it.

CHAPTER 5

Poppy Talks to Junior

JUNIOR DID NOT GET BACK until dark. As usual, he came in and headed right down to root level without saying a word about where he had been or what he'd done. Poppy followed.

Junior's corner was the way it always was, a mess. Poppy had given up trying to get him to clean. Junior wouldn't. Twigs and leaves lay scattered. His bedding, a pile of wood chips, was in total disarray. Junior himself was on his back, paws behind his head, staring glumly up.

Seeing him there, Poppy felt suddenly shy. It was a strange sensation: she had done much in her life, had real adventures—even dangerous ones. How could she be so unsure of herself with her own child? But though Junior was her son, she felt as if she were approaching a complete stranger, someone—how painful to think it—

who could hurt her feelings. Badly.

"Hi," she said, approaching him cautiously.

Junior did not bother to look at her. "What's up?" he said.

"Did you have a pleasant time with Mephitis?"

"Yeah. Sick."

"I'm glad," said Poppy.

"You don't like him."

"Junior, I've never said that. I just don't know him very well."

"Well, he's my freaking best friend."

"What are his parents like?"

"If you're so interested in them, go visit."

"Perhaps I should. But Junior, I didn't come down here to talk about your friend."

"Good."

"Did you have supper?"

"Yes." To prove it, he belched.

"I wish you wouldn't do that. It's very unpleasant."

Junior belched again.

Poppy winced. Then she said, "As you heard me say before, I need to go back with my sister to my old home."

"I hate her."

"Why?"

"She doesn't like me."

"How do you know?"

"Just do."

"I haven't said to the other children what I'm about to tell you, Junior. My father seems to be in a really bad way."

"Rucks to be him," Junior muttered.

Poppy's tail twitched as she waited for Junior to say something more. When he did not, she took a deep breath and then said, "I suppose that between a child and a parent, there is something . . . special. At least," she added, "I feel that way. So, since he is my father, it's important that I go back."

"Okay, Mama," said Junior. "Get to your point."

"Can't you show a little respect for my feelings?"

"Sorry. What is it?"

"Well," said Poppy, working hard to keep her anger down, "as I said, I'll be going back. Leaving tomorrow morning. But your papa and I don't think I should take the whole family." Poppy hesitated but then said, "Junior, I thought I'd ask you to come along with me. Just you. I'd enjoy your company. And it would be good to have someone with me when I came back. Traveling alone through Dimwood can be risky. What do you think?"

"You mean you need me to take care of you."

"I can take care of myself, thank you," said Poppy, struggling to hold back hot tears.

Junior was quiet for a moment. Then he said, "Can Mephitis come?"

"Mephitis?" cried Poppy, taken aback.

"Yeah, Mephitis. What's wrong with that?"

"Why should he come?"

"I told you: he's my best friend."

"But I thought it would be only the two of us. . . ."

"Hey, Mama, I'm not going unless he can come."

Poppy stared at him. "Not even for . . . me?"

"Nope."

"Fine," said Poppy, swallowing her disappointment. "It's a deal. I look forward to getting to know your friend."

Wiping away a tear as she went, Poppy joined the others. Aunt Lilly was telling the rapt children stories about what Poppy was like when she was much younger—how sweet and easy she was.

Rye drew Poppy aside. "What did Junior say?"

"I guess he said yes."

"Only guess?"

"He'll come, but only if Mephitis can come with us."

"Mephitis?"

"I said yes."

"But . . . why?"

"It just . . . feels like the right thing to do."

Rye sighed. "Why did we name him Ragweed Junior? Maybe we shouldn't have."

"Rye, you remember: as soon as he was born, he acted different from the others, doing things his way. Just like Ragweed."

"Maybe a little too different for his own good," said Rye.

Later that night Poppy told Lilly that Junior would travel with them. She didn't have the heart to mention Mephitis.

"Forgive me," said Lilly. "Which one is Junior?"

"The one . . . the one who's dyed black."

"Oh. Poppy, why did he do that?"

"He wants to look like his friend."

"Who is his friend?"

"Mephitis. A . . . skunk."

"A skunk!"

"Lilly," said Poppy, "I like to respect my children's choices."

"Is Junior his whole name?"

"It's Ragweed Junior."

"What I remember about Ragweed is how obnoxious he was. Always asking questions. Never satisfied with anything."

"Lilly, Junior is a good mouse."

Lilly sniffed. "Papa never liked Ragweed. Or porcupines."

"Let's not talk about that," said Poppy.

"Poppy," said Lilly, "you do know Papa has never gotten over your leaving Gray House."

Poppy drew herself up. "Well, I have."

Lilly was silent for a moment. "Poppy, you should know that with . . . Junior looking *that* way—and with *that* name—Papa might get all stirred up."

"I can't help that."

"But Poppy," said Lilly, "you can. Your Rye is very . . . pleasant. And your children are very . . . nice. If a bit . . . excitable."

"Lilly," said Poppy, "is there *anything* about my family you like?"

"Pipsissewa—do I have that name right?—is very cute."

"Lilly, everything will be fine," said Poppy, not sure she meant it.

Feeling the need for some fresh air, she asked Rye to take a walk with her. As they strolled in the night air, she repeated her talk with Lilly.

"Oh, Rye," she said, "I know perfectly well I don't respect Junior's choices. And I must admit, I'm already regretting this trip. It makes me very uneasy."

"Why?"

"Because," said Poppy, "Lilly has reminded me of something."

"What's that?"

"How badly I got along with *my* parents."

CHAPTER 6

Junior and His Friend

AFTER POPPY LEFT HIM, Junior lay on his bed of chips for a while. His mother had made him angry—again. She never noticed that he was no longer a baby, that he had changed, grown older. Agitated, he got up and headed out of the snag.

"Hey, Junior, where you going?" his sister Verbena called.

"None of your business."

"Bet I do know where you're going," she said, sticking her tongue out at him. "To see Mephitis. Which is all you ever do."

Junior gave her a dirty look and hurried away, heading for the path that would take him to Mephitis's house. It was dark, but he knew the path well. Even so, he went slowly, trying to push away his annoyance. He resented the fact that his mother had asked him—and him alone—to go with her when she went to visit her family. He was sure

they would not like him. He could tell Aunt Lilly didn't like him just from the way she looked at him. Probably because he had dyed himself. Too bad for her. Well, he had no intention of liking them, either.

The thing was, whenever Poppy talked about her family—which wasn't often—she mostly mentioned things she had done with her brothers and sisters, or her cousins. Rarely did she say anything about her parents. Or herself. She seemed to have had some kind of problem with them, not that Junior knew what it was. Probably some stupid thing.

It was not like that with his papa. Rye often talked fondly about *his* family. They had even made a few trips to visit them. Rye's old riverside home was fun, with plenty to do. Some of those cousins were cool.

Poppy, however, came from someplace outside Dimwood Forest, somewhere called Gray House. As far as Junior was concerned, the world beyond the forest had to be weird. Why would anyone want to live there? He was sure he would hate it. What's more, Poppy's parents were probably very old. Junior didn't like old mice, finding them creepy and crabby.

He stopped in his tracks. Suddenly he knew why Poppy had asked him to go along: she didn't trust him. Taking him along was some kind of punishment for being what he was. Which meant she was treating him like a baby. Junior felt his anger rising again, but with it came a plan.

When they got to that Gray House, he and Mephitis would do outrageous stuff, stuff so big and so bad, that family would never forget. It would serve them—and his mother—right.

As he approached Mephitis's house, he could smell his friend. It was a pretty strong smell, something Junior admired a lot. You always knew when Mephitis was coming.

But what he liked best was that the skunk was so sure of himself. Mephitis always did what he wanted. No one told him what he could or could not do. He never complained about his parents—never even talked about them.

"Yo, skunk," called Junior as Mephitis came into view.

"Hey," said Mephitis. Compared to Junior, the skunk was large, with thick, black fur and a wide, white stripe that ran from his ears to his large and bushy tail. His pointed snout, ending in his small, black nose, was constantly sniffing. Short legs made him waddle when he walked,

which he did slowly and deliberately. As for his eyes, they were very bright, very much on the alert, as if always on the lookout for anything bad that might come his way.

"Where you going?" Junior asked him.

"Your place."

"What's happening?"

"Nothing."

"Same with me," said Junior. "It's so boring around here."

"Same old same old," agreed Mephitis.

"Hey, guess what?" said Junior.

"What?"

"My old mouse has to go visit her family, and she says I have to go with her."

"How come?"

"She doesn't trust me."

"For how long?"

"Not sure," said Junior. "But I said I'd go on only one condition."

"Yeah, what?"

"You come with us."

"*Me?*"

"Yeah."

The skunk fluffed his tail. "Sick," he said.

"Really sick," agreed Junior. "The thing is, my mother is so boring. I mean she does nothing. Like, she's what? A mother? And there's her sister Lilly. She came to get Mama, so if I went I'd have to go with two old people. Bor-ing. And this place they are going, it's going to be pathetic."

"Rucks to be you."

"Exactly. But if you came, it would be wicked. We could do sick stuff. My mother's family, they don't live in Dimwood, so they don't know nothing. We'd teach them a few things."

"That okay with your mama?" asked Mephitis. "I mean, my coming?"

"I didn't exactly ask her," said Junior with a grin. "I told her. What about your parents? Do you have to ask them?"

"Hey, mouse, you know me: I do what I want."

"Then you'll come?"

Mephitis lifted a paw. Junior slapped it.

"Be ugly!" said Junior.

"Better than ugly, dude," said Mephitis. "Bad."

CHAPTER 7

Leaving

NEXT MORNING POPPY and Rye were up before daylight, going over family arrangements and special problems: Pipsissewa had an earache. Scrub Oak had to be reminded about his chores. Walnut needed to study his lessons more than he had been doing. Locust should be urged not to stay up too late reading the stars. Most importantly: when did Poppy hope she would return?

"As soon as possible," she said. "I promise."

"I'll be right here—waiting," said Rye. "Are you really taking Mephitis?" he asked.

"If he's here on time. If not, I'll go without him."

"And if Junior then decides not to go?"

"At least I've tried."

"I know you have," said Rye, giving her a nuzzle. "Actually, I think Junior went off to fetch Mephitis."

"I suppose I should have spoken to that skunk's parents," said Poppy.

"Too late now. But maybe you'd better tell Ereth you're leaving. You know how much he worries about you."

Agreeing, Poppy went down the path to Ereth's log. "Ereth!" she called. "Are you home?"

"Asparagus teeth!" came a reply from deep inside the log. "Of course I'm home. Where else would I be?"

Poppy smiled and went into the dim, foul-smelling log. Ereth was there, sucking on his lump of salt, now no bigger than an acorn. When she appeared, he barely looked up. All he said was "Have you any idea how good salt is?"

"Ereth, I'll be going away for a while."

Ereth looked up. "Where?"

"I'm afraid my father isn't well. That's why Lilly came.

I need to go see him."

"What the bat bilge for?"

"Really, Ereth, I would think it's obvious. Lungwort is my father. He's elderly. If he's not well, I need to see him. Wouldn't you go see your father if he were ill?"

"No."

"Well, I'm different."

"You once told me you didn't like your father," said Ereth. "Remember that time we planted a tree in honor of Ragweed—the first Ragweed? It was right near your father's house. We didn't even see him."

"Because my father didn't like Ragweed."

"Or porcupines."

"Ereth, my father may be difficult, but . . ."

"But what?"

"Ereth, I believe children owe something to parents. My parents raised me. Cared for me. Protected me. Fed me. Looked after me."

"Poppy," said Ereth, "Junior isn't here. You can turn down the vomit volume. You told me Lungwort made life miserable for you. Restricted you. Always wanted to keep you in your place."

"That was then, and . . ."

"Has anything changed?"

Poppy shrugged. "I hope so."

"Since when do parents get free passes?"

"Ereth, I'm going."

"When?"

"This morning. Right now."

"Now?"

"Yes, with Lilly and—"

"And?"

"Junior."

"Junior! Grumpy goat galoshes. What a picnic. Anyone else?"

"Mephitis."

"The skunk?" cried Ereth.

Poppy nodded.

"Let me get this right: you are going to go home with your sister who talks like a grammar book, your son who is rude, and a skunk you don't like, to your father you can't stand. Have I got it all?"

"Yes," said Poppy.

"Fried Frisbee freckles!" cried Ereth. "This is as brainless as half-baked bagpipes. What are you punishing yourself for?"

Poppy closed her eyes.

"Besides," the porcupine demanded, "who is going to protect you?"

"Oh goodness, Ereth, that's silly."

"I'm going with you."

"No, Ereth, you will not," Poppy said quickly. "First of all, I can protect myself. Second, this is a private family matter. I'm not interested in leading a parade. Besides, you need to stay here and help Rye. Now good-bye. I'll be back soon." With that, Poppy reached up on her hind legs, gave Ereth a quick kiss on the tip of his nose, then hurried away.

Ereth stared cross-eyed at his nose.

Poppy headed back toward the snag and was halfway there when she saw Mephitis and Junior. They were so alike in looks, yet so different in size, that Poppy almost laughed.

Poppy considered the skunk. She really did not know anything about him. She didn't even know where he lived, or who his parents were, or how Junior and he had become friends—or why, for that matter. She had tried to talk to the skunk, but Mephitis was not given to small talk. Since he couldn't fit into the snag, more often than not Junior spent his time at the skunk's house. Once again Poppy regretted never having gone over to introduce herself to Mephitis's parents.

As she drew closer to the snag, she saw that Rye and the children had gathered to say good-bye. Lilly was waiting, too, but as Poppy arrived she saw that her sister's whiskers were stiff and her tail twitching.

"Poppy, can I speak to you for a moment—privately?" Lilly asked.

The two sisters went off a few steps. "Poppy," said Lilly, her lips pursed and her paws folded tightly, "is that . . . skunk coming along?"

Out of the corner of her eye, Poppy could see that Mephitis was watching them. She said, "He and Junior are best friends."

"Frankly," Lilly said, "I don't think it wise. He seems rather . . . surly."

"He'll be fine," said Poppy, wishing she believed it. She broke away from Lilly and went up to the skunk. "Mephitis, I understand you want to go with us?"

Mephitis pointed his sharp nose to the ground. When he and Poppy met, which was not often, he usually dropped his tail and looked anywhere but at her. It made Poppy feel uncomfortable—as if the skunk were hiding something.

"I guess," he murmured, as much to the ground as to her.

"I'm very glad you're coming," Poppy forced herself to say. "And . . . is it all right with your parents?"

"Come on, Mama," called Junior. "Don't be so freaking nosey." He turned to his friend and belched. The skunk grinned, and the two slapped paws over Poppy's head.

Poppy winced and started to say something more, but decided she didn't want to begin the trip in an even worse mood. Instead, she looked around. She caught Rye's gaze. He winked. It made Poppy smile.

"I guess it's time to go," she said in her best chirpy squeak.

Rye lined the children up in a row. Poppy went down the line, hugging and nuzzling each one, giving final bits of advice:

"Pipsissewa, please help your father. Walnut, a little less squabbling with your sisters. Snowberry, don't forget to wash your face. Verbena, do clean up after yourself. . . ."

Last in line was Rye. "Please be safe," he whispered into Poppy's ear as he gave her a hug. "Don't worry about us. We'll be perfectly fine. Send my regards to your family, especially your father."

Poppy turned to whisper into Rye's right ear, the one that bore a little notch from a childhood accident, which somehow made it Poppy's favorite. "I'll try to make this as fast as I possibly can," she promised.

"Just remember," he said with a final hug, "your family will be waiting right here for you."

"I'll miss you," Poppy whispered.

"And I you."

Poppy turned about and looked at Lilly and Junior, as well as Mephitis. "Well then," she said, more brightly than she felt, "here we go."

Off she started with Lilly at her side and Junior and Mephitis trailing behind.

"Ga-ba, ga-ba, good-bye!" cried all the other children as well as Rye. "Good-bye!"

They watched and called until the traveling party had disappeared into the woods. Rye was the last to turn away. Just as he did, he saw Ereth come rushing down the path from his log.

"Zappy zit jelly!" cried the porcupine. "Has Poppy already gone?"

"They just left."

"Which way?"

"Down that path."

"Fine. I'm going with them," cried Ereth. "Don't touch my salt!" With that, he trundled after the travelers.

"Ereth!" Rye called. "Come back!" But Ereth was out of sight.

CHAPTER 8

Through
Dimwood Forest

POPPY AND LILLY, followed by Junior and Mephitis, hiked along a narrow game trail through Dimwood Forest. The early morning sun, low in the sky, filtered down through the tall pine trees, splashing the ground and earth-hugging bushes with warmth in shades of yellow and orange. Here and there flowers—like lost coins, gold, white, and red—flashed. Unseen birds jabbered and whistled, the flutter of their wings signaling the unfolding of a new day. The forest fragrance, a blend of the sweetly living and the sweetly dying, filled the senses.

Lilly, however, felt tense. It was hard enough to think of her father, Lungwort, being ill. That he had sent for Poppy rather than ask Lilly to solve the problems at Gray House was painful. She privately had hoped Poppy would not come. Not only was Poppy coming, but she was bringing a rude child by the name of Ragweed! As for the skunk, that was beyond even thinking about. Lilly tried to distract herself by collecting pine seeds, knowing her father had a fondness for them. She kept the seeds in a folded leaf.

Junior was nervous. Within a short time they had moved farther away from the snag than he had ever gone before. The forest was larger, deeper, and darker than he had imagined. For the first time he understood why it was called Dimwood. Feeling quite puny, Junior was grateful that Mephitis was at his side, so large and confident. To hide his unease, Junior talked, but most of all he laughed. To laugh meant everything was all right.

Mephitis was glad he was with Junior, too. He depended on the mouse's constant sense of fun, his ready laughter, and his lack of worry. Yes, Junior liked to complain about his parents, taking for granted that they were always there to complain about. Mephitis loved to hear about Junior's large family—not that he ever said so. Nor did he want to get too close to them. If they learned the truth about him, they might forbid him Junior's company. That would be awful.

As Poppy gazed about at the forest, she could only smile. She was recalling with fond amusement how her first view of the forest had filled her with awe. Since then, not only had she come to love Dimwood Forest, she adored the life of adventures and surprises she discovered there. Even as she walked, she caught sight of a spiderweb. It was wet with dew, glistening in the early sunlight—simultaneously delicate yet strong. Then she found herself thinking of Rye, the children, and Ereth. Her thoughts kept the smile on her face. If she had been alone, she might have danced.

Instead, as she and Lilly walked side by side, Poppy set the pace, eager to complete the trip, then return home. Lilly was more careful in her steps. From behind, Poppy could hear Mephitis and Junior's chatter. While she could not tell what they were saying, they continually broke out into boisterous laughter. A few times they exchanged belches, which evoked even more laughter. While Poppy was glad they were having such a good time—she loved their youthful exuberance—it saddened her that Junior laughed so much with his skunk friend but had stopped doing so with her. There was a time, not so long ago, that he had laughed a lot with her. To laugh with your own children—nothing was better!

"I must confess," Lilly said to Poppy, breaking into her thoughts, "as delightful as was my brief visit to Dimwood Forest, I'm glad to be going home. I'm sure you're pleased to be going home, too—at last."

"I've come to think of the snag as my home," said Poppy.

"Goodness!" said her sister. "That old dead tree? Poppy, it doesn't even have branches. You surprise me. I thought you had more style."

Poppy thought for a moment before saying, "Lilly, it's where my family lives."

"Oh, I know," said Lilly with a light laugh. "And I suppose you probably do *need* to live there. Still, I believe there's nothing like one's *old* home—*old* family. Don't misunderstand me, Poppy. Rye seems devoted to you. I'm sure he's a good husband. I found him very pleasant. Very accommodating. But then, after all, he is, well . . . a *golden* mouse. I'm sure it will be so nice for you to be among what's most familiar—and comfortable—your own kind. The deer mice with whom you grew up. That has to be . . . well . . . restful. I'm sure you can stay as long as you like. Mama is so looking forward to your visit. No need to hurry back. Rye seems quite competent."

Poppy, trying to decide if Lilly was trying to be funny, stole a glance at her sister. In the end she realized Lilly was simply saying what she believed. Poppy decided it would be best if she changed the subject. "Why are you collecting those seeds?" she asked.

"For Papa. He finds them soothing. And I like doing things for him."

"How long," asked Poppy when that topic went

nowhere, "did it take you to get from Gray House to my place?"

"Most of a day," said Lilly. "But once you get across Glitter Creek, it's nothing."

"Was the water up?" Poppy asked. Mention of the creek reminded her how she first had crossed it a long time ago—short rock-to-rock leaps, during which she had slipped into the water and almost drowned.

"I took the bridge," said Lilly. "Now that the dreadful owl—what was his name?"

"Do you mean Mr. Ocax?"

"Right, Ocax. . . . Now that he has left the neighborhood, getting about is *so* much easier. But Poppy," Lilly went on, "I should warn you: you'll find Lungwort changed."

"How so?"

"He's not very strong. He spends a lot of time in that old boot of his, sleeping. Not that he wants to give up his authority as the head of the family. You know Lungwort: change is the enemy. So he does complain a lot and is easily agitated."

"He always was agitated," said Poppy.

"I suppose," said Lilly. "And it's that which makes me offer a suggestion."

"Which is?"

"It's about that skunk—Junior's friend. What's his name?"

"Mephitis."

"Yes, something odd. While, I will admit, I wish he wasn't coming along with us, I trust he doesn't have to actually, well, you know, actually come *into* Gray House. It would be . . . distressing. To Papa, surely. And everyone else. Skunks, well, smell. And, have you noticed, he belches a lot."

Poppy stopped walking and faced her sister squarely, pink nose to pink nose. "Lilly," she said, "you may be my sister. But you are a snob."

Lilly laughed lightly. "Now Poppy, *someone* has to keep up the old standards!"

"I'm afraid you and I have different standards." Upset, Poppy let her sister move ahead and waited until Junior and Mephitis caught up to her.

As soon as the youngsters saw that Poppy was waiting for them, they became quiet. "How are you getting along?" she asked them.

"That's a stupid question," said Junior.

Poppy, ignoring Junior's remark, said, "Mephitis, have you traveled much?"

"Nope." He avoided looking at her.

"It was nice of your parents to allow you to come along. I know Junior appreciates it."

"Yeah."

"I should like to meet them some day."

The skunk lifted his tale and waved it, but didn't reply.

"Have you any brothers or sisters?"

"Guess so."

"Only guess?"

"Haven't seen them in a while."

"Why is that?"

"Mama," cried Junior, "do you have to be so nosey all the time?"

"Junior," said Poppy, "I'm just trying to get to know your friend a little better."

"That's okay," said Mephitis to Junior. "See," he said to Poppy, glancing at her before averting his eyes again, "I don't see my brother or sister because I don't live at home."

"You don't?"

"Nope."

"Then whom do you live with?"

The skunk shrugged. "I'm . . . on my own."

Poppy stopped. "Are you saying you don't live with your parents?"

Mephitis shook his head.

"Why is that?"

"Because," cried Junior, "he's lazy, spoiled, self-centered, and a bad influence on everybody. All he does is make trouble and a lot of mess, so no one ought to have to put up with him."

"I also stink too much," said Mephitis, grinning.

Poppy closed her eyes.

"The way I see it, Miss Poppy," Mephitis went on, "families are old stuff."

"Aren't you glad you asked?" Junior said to Poppy.

"Mephitis, it seems to me—," Poppy began to say, only to decide such talk was useless. Instead, she turned away and walked alone, her good mood completely gone.

CHAPTER 9

Something Ahead

I T WAS LILLY, walking in the lead, who was the first to realize that something unusual lay ahead. When Poppy caught up to her, she had stopped walking and was standing tall on her hind legs, her whiskers twitching as she sniffed.

"What's the matter?" said Poppy.

"Shhh!" Lilly whispered. "Ahead of us. I don't know what it is, but it's not right."

"What is it?"

"Listen."

Poppy did so, her pink tail stiff with tension, her large ears shifted forward. What she heard was the sound of bushes being tossed and broken. A musky smell filled the air.

"What do you think it is?" said Lilly.

"I have no idea," said Poppy.

"We need to go a different way," said Lilly, backing up.

"Don't you think we should see what it is first?" said Poppy.

"Don't be foolish, Poppy," snapped Lilly. "It's always better to avoid danger before it happens. We can go a different way."

"But isn't this the most direct trail?" asked Poppy.

Even as they debated, Junior and Mephitis caught up to them. "What's happening?" said Junior. "What are you two arguing about?"

"Shhh!" Lilly said. "There's something ahead."

"You mean the trees?" said Junior.

Mephitis, turning to Junior, laughed and said, "No, the bushes."

"Whooping big fat deal," said Junior with a grin.

"Very whooping big fat deal," said the skunk. He lifted a paw. Junior slapped it. That brought more laughter.

"You are both acting immature and unenlightened!" said Lilly. "I am not going another inch forward."

"Then stay here," said Poppy. "I'll go and check."

"Yeah," said Junior. "Me, too."

"You will *not*," said Poppy. "You'll stay here until I see what it is."

"Stop treating me like a baby," said Junior.

"I'll stop when you stop acting like one," Poppy returned. "Now stay!"

Junior muttered something under his breath that Poppy was glad she did not hear. But she did hear Lilly say, "Poppy, as always, you are taking unnecessary risks and putting us in jeopardy."

Poppy bristled. "I like taking risks," she snapped. "I'll be right back." As she went, she glanced back to make sure the others remained behind. "So silly, all of them," she said aloud, not caring if they heard. Then she put her mind to what lay ahead.

The trail, which was quite narrow, went straight for a few yards and then looped around a tree. Beyond that it took another sharp turn around a boulder, all of which made it impossible to see ahead very far. Poppy crept along carefully, her pink nose up, sniffing. Her legs—even as they carried her forward—were poised to spring back and flee.

The farther Poppy went, the stronger was the smell she had detected. Without question it was an animal smell, but not one Poppy knew right away. What's more, as she went on, the sounds grew louder. It occurred to her that whatever was around the bend was more than one creature.

She paused and wondered if her sister might be right—if she was too much of a risk taker. *No*, she thought. *I am not going to let Lilly tell me how to act.*

Resolved, Poppy crept forward. When she spied a tangle of roots by the side of the path, she threaded her way through. That brought her around the bend. After making sure she was hidden, she poked her head up.

Seated in the middle of the path ahead was a bear.

CHAPTER 10

The Bears

To POPPY'S EYES, the bear, cinnamon brown in color with a patch of white splashed on her chest, was enormous, quite the largest animal Poppy ever had seen in Dimwood Forest. Not nearly so huge—but big enough—was the bear cub tumbling about between his mother's legs. The cub was in a flurry of motion, climbing awkwardly on his mother only to tumble down and dart away, then to dash back, trip, hug his mother, and give her a lick before tumbling off again, but never too far.

Poppy might have found mother and infant cub a charming scene if it had not been so terrifying. Bears, she knew, were perfectly willing to eat mice.

As it was, she stared at the bears a moment too long. The little bear spied her, too. Bright brown eyes very large, mouth partly open, pink tongue extended, the cub gawked at Poppy, as if not believing what he was seeing, as if he had never seen such a little creature before. Poppy, captivated by the bear's childish, comical expression, looked back.

The next moment the cub made a sudden leap to where Poppy was lodged. Poppy ducked just in time. But the cub, squealing and chuffing, stuck his drippy nose deep among the roots. Poppy squirmed away, only to find herself squeezed against another root, one she could not pass.

The cub shoved a paw down among the roots, close to Poppy. Heart hammering, Poppy pressed herself as flat as her spine would allow against a root. The cub's claws stroked down her furry side. It was close but harmless. Still, Poppy knew it was only a matter of time before the cub did her real damage.

She looked for a way to escape, saw a small hole, dived into it, then scratched her way up, only to come up against the cub's snorting wet nose again. Once more she dived, dropping into a crevice bounded by roots on three sides. With the excited cub clumping all about, pawing wildly, Poppy was momentarily safe—but trapped. She told herself to be patient: the cub would grow tired and back off. Instead, the cub began squealing, "Mama! Mama! Look!"

To Poppy's horror, the mother bear rose up and lum-

bered over to see what was so interesting to her cub. Each step she took made the ground tremble.

"Help!" squealed Poppy in her highest voice. "Help!" Whom she was calling, she had no. idea. She had told Junior to stay behind.

"All right, Brutus," said the big bear as she came up to her cub. "What do you have there?"

"I don't know what you call it," said the cub.

"Let me see," said the mother bear. She thrust her large black nose deep down among the roots very close to Poppy—so close her strong breath made Poppy gag. While the bear couldn't quite reach her, Poppy could see her yellow teeth. There were a lot of them, all long and jagged.

The mother bear withdrew her snout. "Brutus," she informed her cub, "what you have caught is a mouse."

"Can I eat it?"

"If you want to. But you've only trapped it. Now you have to catch it."

"How do I do that?" cried the little bear, hardly able to contain his excitement.

"Now Brutus, be patient. That bitty thing isn't going anywhere, so just keep clawing and scratching. You'll get to it soon enough. If it tries to run off, just slap it with your paw. That will kill it, but you can still eat it."

"Can you show me how, Mama?"

"Of course I can. What you do is . . . oh my, what do we have here?" She turned about. So did the cub.

Poppy, taken equally by surprise, managed to look around. Mephitis was trotting around the bend. Riding just behind the skunk's head was Junior. The young mouse called, "Hey, Mama, where are you?"

"Is that . . . mouse calling you 'mama'?" the cub asked.

"No, Brutus, honey, I'm not the mouse's mother. . . . Now come here with me."

"Why?" said the cub. "Why can't I play with that large one, too?" He bounded toward Mephitis.

"Brutus!" cried the mother bear. "Don't!"

It was too late. As Brutus tumbled toward Mephitis, the skunk swiveled around, stood up on his forepaws, aimed his backside, and sprayed a double cloud of stink. The cub took it right in his face.

"Yipes!" he shrieked.

Trying to reverse his forward rush, the cub thrust out his paws and skittered to such a sudden halt that he tumbled forward, did a somersault, and landed flat on his back. "Mama!" he screamed. "Mama! It stinks! It stinks!"

The mother bear rushed forward, only to be met by a second smelly squirt from Mephitis.

With a roar, the bear smacked the skunk to one side, sending Junior flying in a different direction. Without pause she scooped up the squealing cub and went crashing through the woods as fast as she could go.

Poppy, even as the rank cloud of skunk stink descended on her, jumped out from the roots calling, "Junior! Where are you? Are you hurt?"

CHAPTER II

A Question
of Bathing

A RAUCOUSLY LAUGHING JUNIOR crawled out from the bushes. "Skunk," he cried, "you are totally ugly sick!"

"Did I get them both?" said a grinning Mephitis as he reappeared on the path.

"You certainly did, and I thank you," cried Poppy, rather breathless as she checked herself all over from head to tail.

Junior and Mephitis met mid-trail and slapped paws. "Skunk," proclaimed Junior, "you have the sickest stink in the world! Ultimate wicked."

"You ain't so good yourself, mouse," returned his friend, laughing just as loudly.

"That little bear almost caught me," said Poppy. "Then I thought he was going to get you."

Junior's smile got bigger even as he wrinkled his nose.

"What's the matter?" said Poppy.

"Little Mama," said Junior, "no offense, but you stink. I mean, nasty stink." He began to laugh again.

Poppy, smiling weakly, sniffed. "You don't smell so good, either."

Mephitis, nodding, said, "Miss Poppy, I'm afraid you've turned into a skunk."

"Well, I wasn't eaten," said Poppy. "Thanks to you."

"I guess my stink can pretty well chase anything away."

"This skunk," said Junior, crawling back up to take his seat on the skunk's head, "is one smelly dude—even for a skunk. But it was me who heard you calling, Mama. Good thing I didn't stay back the way you told me to, right?"

"I suppose so," Poppy felt obliged to say.

"See," proclaimed Junior, greatly enjoying himself, "a mouse has to do what a mouse has to do! And what he has to do is protect his wimpy old mama!"

A breathless Lilly burst upon the trail. "Good gracious," she cried. "There you are. I was so worried. What in the world was all that— Oh, my heavens!" she cried, slapping a paw to her nose. "What *is* that smell?"

"It's my buddy Mephitis," said Junior.

"Why, it's absolutely . . . revolting," said Lilly. She hurried past the skunk toward Poppy, only to stop. "Poppy!

I'm afraid you, too . . . have a very bad . . . odor."

"Don't you even want to know what happened?" said Poppy.

"It's fairly obvious—this malodorous skunk sprayed you."

"Actually," said Poppy, "this very brave skunk saved me from a bear."

Mephitis grinned.

"A bear!" cried Lilly. "Here? Attacking?"

"I'm afraid so."

"This forest is perfectly hateful," said Lilly. "And even if Mephitis did save you, he might have done it with greater consideration for others. Really, Poppy," she said, "this is all quite awful."

"Lilly, didn't you hear me? Mephitis saved my life."

"As they say," said Lilly, "there are worse things than death. Now Poppy, as soon as we get to Glitter Creek you must wash yourself off. You, too, Junior. Thoroughly. I mean, you cannot—you must not—come home smelling like that."

"Yo, Mama," said Junior, "think what you would say if I came home smelling so bad."

"You are all—!" Poppy, unable to decide what word to use, turned about and marched down the trail thinking, *I don't know whether to laugh or cry.*

I can't wait till I get home, thought Lilly.

This forest is dangerous, thought Junior.

She called me brave, thought Mephitis.

But nobody spoke a word.

CHAPTER 12

On the Banks of Glitter Creek

POPPY, IN THE LEAD, kept to herself. Lilly came next. Junior, riding on Mephitis's back again, was last. Though Poppy and Lilly remained silent, Junior and Mephitis quickly resumed their laughter and loud chatter. Mostly they talked about bad smells they had encountered—arguing loudly about who had smelled the worst stench. Junior recalled a mess of rotting stinkweed. Mephitis had once come upon a clutch of broken bird eggs—two weeks old. Junior countered with a tale of a stagnant pond filled with dead fish. Mephitis topped all with a tale about a field of elk poop. Poppy tried hard not to listen to this truly revolting conversation. But once or twice she caught herself grinning. They were, she had to admit, funny in their way, even though Poppy was certain she and her best friend and cousin, Basil, had never, ever talked about such things when they were young.

It was noon when Poppy reached the edge of the forest and stood on the banks of Glitter Creek. The water was not nearly so turbulent as it had been when she crossed it the first time, so long ago. Now the creek was almost languid in its movement, though here and there the water frothed and foamed. Elsewhere it twirled in gurgling whirlpools, even as the creek babbled around and between rocks and logs. Dragonflies hovered low, wings a blur, before darting off in bursts of nervous energy. In contrast, a turtle, having found a sunlit rock, sat utterly still, dreaming its torpid turtle dreams.

Poppy had forgotten what it was like not to be beneath the trees of Dimwood. The bright sun dazzled her, making her a little dizzy. Overhead the blue sky, with its high-flying birds and drifting clouds, was like another realm. The smells were lighter than in the forest. Here the breezy air carried now this scent, now another, in a shifting kaleidoscope of gentle nose-tickling sensations.

As Poppy absorbed it all, the thought came to her that the creek was like a boundary. On one side, where she stood, was the edge of Dimwood Forest. On the far side was open land—a very different world. Poppy felt a moment of panic. The creek also marked the dividing line between her past and her present. Did she really want to

return to the past? She had barely considered the notion when Lilly came out of the woods.

Poppy's sister—as she had done since the smelly encounter with the bears—kept her distance, going so far as to make sure she stayed upwind, and being very obvious about it.

"I'm so glad," she announced, "to be out from all that forest gloom and stench. Now all we have to do is cross the creek and go through the Old Orchard, and we'll be at Gray House. I think that when we get across the creek and climb the bank, we'll be able to see it."

Poppy, feeling quite emotional and wishing she were alone, said only, "I don't recall."

Lilly sniffed. "Poppy," she said, "aren't you going to bathe?"

"Maybe," said Poppy. She had been intending to wash herself, but she didn't want it to appear she was doing so at her sister's bidding. Instead, she sat by the water's edge, put her paw in the water, and dabbled about. "The water is quite warm," she said.

"What do you mean, 'maybe' you'll take a bath?" demanded Lilly. "Poppy, the two of you *cannot* come home smelling the way you do. It would be disrespectful. Really, you smell horrible, which is something only your sister could tell you."

"Lilly," Poppy returned, while continuing to gaze upon the flowing water, "that is something only my sister *would* tell me."

Mephitis and Junior tumbled out of the woods. "Hey, a creek," cried Junior. "Who wants to go swimming?" He did not wait for a reply, but slid off the skunk's back and plunged into the water.

"Young mouse!" cried Lilly. "You are splashing me!"

Junior's response was to slap the water hard with a paw, sending a water spray right at his aunt.

She jumped away, crying, "Poppy, tell him to stop!"

Poppy, speaking softly and with a hint of a smile said, "Junior, do stop."

"Okay," said Junior, with an understanding grin. He began to swim about. Mephitis joined him, and the two frolicked.

Lilly watched them for a moment. Then she said, "Poppy, I've decided something."

"What is that?"

"I think I'll go downstream a bit, take the bridge across, and get on home. First. That way I can tell them you're coming. You and Junior can take your time."

"What you mean, Lilly," said Poppy, "is that you want to warn them about me."

"Poppy," said Lilly, "Papa is easily agitated."

"Then go right ahead and un-agitate him," said Poppy. "We'll come along soon."

"Fine," said Lilly, and she started off along the edge of the creek. She hadn't gone far before she stopped and looked back. "Poppy, promise me you and Junior will bathe."

"Actually," said Poppy. "I'm going to ask Mephitis to give us another dose of his stink."

"Poppy, you wouldn't!" squealed Lilly.

"No," said Poppy with a rueful smile. "But I'd like to."

Lilly hesitated, as if wanting to say something, before moving off. This time she did not look back.

As Lilly disappeared around a bend, Poppy sighed with disappointment. The truth was, she was not liking her sister very much. The next moment Poppy gave herself a mental scolding: *Lilly is just being who she is,* she felt obliged to acknowledge.

"You know who you and Lilly remind me of," called Junior when he saw that his aunt had left.

"Who?"

"Me and my sister Columbine."

"That's ridiculous," said Poppy.

"Nope! We're just the same," insisted Junior. "We don't like each other, either. Where's she going?"

"Lilly decided to go ahead, to tell them not to be too upset when they see us—or at least to act as if they aren't upset."

"What are they going to get upset about?" asked Junior.

"Oh . . . it's too complicated to explain," said Poppy. She sat for a moment, thinking about what Junior had said, only to be suddenly doused by a spray of water.

Startled, Poppy looked up. "Ragweed Junior!" she cried out. The next second she caught herself: *I don't want to be angry.* And after all, she really did need to wash. With that thought, she plunged into the creek so abruptly she took Junior by surprise and dunked him.

He came up spluttering, "Hey, Mama," he shouted. "What are you doing?" The next moment he burst out laughing, and the two fought a furious water battle. Looking

on, Mephitis laughed with them, but then joined in on Poppy's side.

"Not fair!" cried a gleeful Junior.

After exhausting themselves, the trio waded out of the creek and lay down in the sun to dry.

"Hey, Mama?" called Junior. "How far do we have to go?"

"It's pretty much what your Aunt Lilly said: cross over the creek, get through the Old Orchard, and Gray House will be right there."

"Cool."

Poppy, eyes closed, lay back in the sun with her furry white belly up. Her whiskers dried quickly. The warmth filled and soothed her. She was thoroughly relaxed when she heard Mephitis whisper, "Hey, Junior, your mother is pretty cool."

"Maybe," said Junior. "But it sure was a good thing we were there for the bear. She's so wimpy. I liked her better when she stunk."

"Yeah," muttered the skunk.

Poppy, not wanting to hear any more of this conversation, sprang up.

"Hey, Mama," Junior called. "Where you going?"

"I think I need to be alone," she said, and walked away along the creek bank.

CHAPTER 13

Junior and Mephitis

Did I say something wrong?" Junior said to Mephitis.

"Don't ask me," said the skunk. "I don't know nothing about parents. I can't ever figure them out."

"Neither can I," said Junior. "All I know is, I'm never going to be like that."

"Like what?"

"Old. It's too weird. Hey, did you hear what my mama said?"

"About what?"

"Aunt Lilly. She decided to go ahead to that Gray House so she could tell them not to be freaked out when they saw us."

"I heard," said the skunk. "But I don't think your aunt was talking about your mama."

"Exactly," said Junior, grinning. "It's *us* she doesn't like." He belched and lifted a paw. Mephitis slapped it.

"Actually," said the skunk, "I think it's *me* she doesn't like."

"Hey, you stink, but I'm rude. Did you see the look on her face when I splashed her?"

The two burst into laughter.

"You still stink," said Mephitis. "Don't you want to wash some more?"

"I'd rather gross them out," said Junior.

The two laughed for so long they started laughing at their own laughing.

"I do like your mama, though," said the skunk when they calmed down. "She's pretty cool."

"Yeah, she's all right," said Junior.

"I wish she were my mother," said Mephitis.

"She can't be," said Junior. "You're a skunk."

"Hey, your uncle's a porcupine."

That brought more laughter.

For a while they were quiet. Then Junior said, "You know what I think we should do?"

"What?"

"Let's get to that house before my Aunt Lilly does. You know, go swaggering in as if we owned the place. Be so totally wicked."

"Fine with me," said the skunk. "There's only one other thing."

"What?"

"You're not black anymore. The soot from the burnt tree you used got washed off in the water."

Junior looked himself over. "Dang! I forgot about that. Maybe I can find something on the other side to dye myself again. Don't want to get there looking ordinary for that family."

Junior waded into the water. Stepping carefully, sometimes swimming, he worked his way across Glitter Creek. Mephitis waddled across. "Oh, NO!" he said when he reached the other side.

"What?" said Junior.

"Your stink is a lot less."

"Can't have that. Do me!" He turned his back on the skunk. Mephitis stood on his forepaws and squirted.

"What do you think?" asked Junior.

Mephitis sniffed. "Beautiful!"

"Come on," said Junior, "up the bank. I think Mama said there's an orchard. Whatever that is. We've got to go through it. Then it'll be that Gray House place."

"Nothing to it." The skunk scrambled up the bank with ease. Once on top, Mephitis and Junior stared at the Old Orchard, which lay before them. Instead of the tall, straight pine trees that grew randomly throughout the forest, the orchard consisted of a few dozen ancient apple trees, spaced evenly one from the other, trunks twisted, branches low and drooping. And the orchard air, unlike the tangy, dry pine smell of the woods, was as sweet and moist as honey and almost as heavy.

"That's some weird forest," said Junior.

"Your ma called it an orchard," Mephitis reminded him.

"Smells sweet. What's that boxy thing way over there?"

"I think that's what they call Gray House," said Junior.

The two gazed at it silently.

"You know what?" said Mephitis.

"What?"

"I never saw a house before. Is that where your family lives?"

"Hey, skunk, not *my* family. My mama's. I never saw any of them 'cept my Aunt Lilly who I just met. Oh yeah, once we came to plant a tree for my dead Uncle Ragweed—the one I'm named after—up on that hill over there, I think. Except my mother didn't want to visit anyone. But I saw

the house from a distance."

"What was your uncle like?"

"Skunk, that mouse did some wild stuff. I mean, really wicked. So they all hated Ragweed—that's what my ma said. 'Specially her father." Junior lowered his voice: " 'A mouse has to do what a mouse has to do.' Ragweed used to say that. Is that cool or what? He only did what he liked."

"What happened to him?"

"Got killed."

"How?"

Junior shrugged. "Dunno. Anyway, he wasn't stiff like that Lilly."

"Just became a stiff," said Mephitis.

"Skunk," said Junior, "if they're all like Aunt Lilly, it'll be nasty. But I don't care. Not really."

"Me, neither."

"The way I see it," said Junior, "if they don't like me, I won't like them just as much. So let's go get 'em."

The two worked their way slowly through the orchard without speaking. Beneath the bright, warm sun, the grass was lush, with many colorful flowers to see and to smell. Apples lay on the ground. Grasshoppers rattled their wings while leaping about at random. Bees droned. Now and again a butterfly fluttered past, while jays, warblers, and bluebirds swooped and scooped up insects in their open maws.

"Freaking nice here," said Junior after a while.

Mephitis grunted his agreement.

They meandered on quietly, pausing occasionally to look back and see how far they had come. But after a while Junior said, "I've been thinking: we could go back and wait for my mama. Could be easier that way."

"Suppose."

"Except, if we went back and she wasn't there, things would get mixed up."

"Right."

"So I guess we better keep going," said Junior. "Maybe she'll be there when we show up—if we go slow enough."

"Hope so," said the skunk.

They went a little farther, until Mephitis said, "You know, I could use a nap."

"Me, too," said Junior. "Anyway, we want to be sure my mama's there first, right?"

By way of answering, Mephitis lay down, curled up, wrapped his bushy tail around his body, and closed his eyes. Junior lay back against his friend, resting his head against Mephitis's soft belly. Then he reached out to pluck a juicy strand of fragrant grass. He chewed it idly. "Yep, pretty nice here," he murmured.

Under the sun's soft warmth and the breezes so gently teasing, the two friends were soon slumbering.

CHAPTER 14

An Old Friend

As JUNIOR AND MEPHITIS NAPPED, a melancholy Poppy walked slowly along the banks of Glitter Creek. Now and again she picked up a pebble and flicked it into the water. She even tried to skip one, but only achieved one jump before the stone sank. "Just like me," she said.

Poppy was disappointed in herself. In her life she had felt anger and calm, fear and courage. She had experienced danger and joy. She had felt love and hate. While she had been bored a few times in her life, she had been excited many more times. But never before had she felt so sad.

Surely Junior was a great frustration, a mystery that should not be a mystery. And she was disappointed in her sister. Was she sad, she wondered, because of her father's aging? Not really. Though she wanted only the best for him, it was, after all, only to be expected. He was an old mouse.

She reminded herself that on the other side of things, there was Rye. She adored him. And there were her children. She loved them so much, including Junior. Yes, he was rude. And crude. But he did have a wonderful laugh. No one could still laugh like that and be bad. And that water fight—it had been fun. Then there was her life in the forest. There was Ereth. It was all so good.

And yet . . . she was sad. What was it, she wondered, about family that made her both happy and sad at the same time?

Poppy continued to wander along the creek bank, the frustration within at odds with the calmly flowing waters by her side. Suddenly she stopped, unwilling to believe what she was seeing. "Erethizon Dorsatum!" she cried. "What are you doing here?"

The old porcupine was sitting by the edge of the creek, scooping water and washing his face. Hearing Poppy's voice, he looked about and grunted, but continued to clean himself without saying anything.

"Ereth," cried Poppy. "Answer me!"

"Mole mucus milkshakes," said Ereth. "Can't you see I'm washing my face?"

"In all the time I've known you, you have *never* washed your face!"

"Then it's about time."

"But why are you even here?"

"Because I want to be, pickle pot. Or do you happen to

own this part of the world?"

"You followed me here, didn't you?"

"If I followed you, bottom brain, I'd be behind you. As you might have noticed, it was you who found me."

"You understand me perfectly well," said Poppy. "You knew where I was going, and even though I asked you not to come, you came anyway."

"I've been looking for some fresh salt."

"And Ereth," said Poppy, "I asked you to stay home and help Rye."

"He can do it himself," muttered Ereth.

"And I can't travel myself? Is that what you're saying?"

"You need protection."

"From what?"

"Your family."

"Ereth, everything is fine."

"Spinach ice cream!" cried Ereth. "What's happened to you?"

"Ereth, nothing has happened to me. I am going to see my father, who is sick. It won't help to have you there."

"Oh, kippered kafuffles! You used to like it when I was around. Have you gotten tired of me?"

"Ereth," cried Poppy, close to tears, "my father does not like porcupines."

"How come?"

"He just doesn't. It's ignorance. And I apologize for it."

"Right!" exploded Ereth. "And we certainly don't want to educate anyone, do we? Don't want the truth to embarrass someone, do we? Which is to say I suppose I'm good enough for some of your friends. Just not good enough for your family. Sure, I thought I'd just stay on the edges of things in case you needed me. Lend a quick quill if necessary. A little help on the side—if needed. Old friends do come in handy, you know. But snot weed sauerkraut, I guess I was wrong. Forget all we've ever done together. Forget the past.

Never mind the future. See you around, fur butt. It's been grand. Lovely! All you have to do is let me know when you want your best friend back, flea jacket, and I'll be right there! Count on me! Forget it, mushroom mouth, forget it! Get yourself a fried earwax sandwich and eat it backward. Good-bye!"

Still spluttering, Ereth spun around and waddled away into the forest.

"Ereth, wait!" cried Poppy. "You don't understand! Please, listen to me. I need to talk to you."

It was too late. Ereth had gone. The old porcupine crashed through the underbrush, prickly tail lashing back and forth with rage. "Petulant pig buttons," he muttered. "Square root of platypus!"

Suddenly he stopped and spun about, looking back. Though he stared at nothing in particular, his thoughts were all on Poppy. It was not as if he thought she was in any physical danger. But she was clearly unhappy. Upset. She couldn't mean what she was saying. She couldn't.

"Buttered bilge on creamed cement!" he swore. "She is *not* going to tell me where I can and can't go! If I want to go visit her family, I'll do it!"

With that, Ereth turned again and started back toward Glitter Creek and the Old Orchard beyond.

★ ★ ★

After Ereth had plunged into the forest, Poppy stared at the place where her friend had gone. As she listened to the rustling noise of the porcupine running through the grass, tears ran down her cheeks and along her pink nose and whiskers. "This," she murmured, "is the most awful time I have ever, ever had. I hate families! Hate them!" Then she sighed. "But there is no choice, is there? I'm part of a family."

Poppy began to walk slowly back along the edge of the creek. She went with her head bowed, her tail drooping, and her heart heavy.

This is ridiculous, she heard herself thinking. *A catastrophe! I should have come alone. If everyone in Gray House is like Lilly, it will be ghastly! They aren't going to like me. Having Junior along is going to make things even worse. No, he cannot go to Gray House with me. He must go home. With Mephitis. I don't care what Junior says. And it's better that Ereth didn't come. This is something I need to do alone. Fine! I'll go to Gray House, pay my respects to Papa, spend a little time with Mama, and then get right back home where I belong.*

So resolved, Poppy made her way along Glitter Creek. But when she got to the place she had left them, she discovered that Junior and Mephitis were gone.

CHAPTER 15

Lilly Reaches Gray House

LILLY HURRIED ALONG THE CREEK as fast as she could go. "What is the matter with Poppy?" she asked herself, quite aloud. "What has happened to her? Yes, she used to be a little headstrong, but now . . ." Lilly shook her head. "Though of course I really do know what the problem is: it's what comes of leaving one's family. Abandoning them. Going off with . . . a . . . a golden mouse. Look at that young Ragweed. So unpleasant! No better than the first Ragweed. And that skunk! Unthinkable! What will Papa say? What will Mama say! What will everyone say? It's *so* embarrassing. As for that horrid, vulgar porcupine, what a catastrophe it would be if *he* showed up! Thank goodness he's not coming! I just hope these pine seeds will soothe Papa."

Lilly had reached the bridge that crossed the creek. It was hardly more than a row of wooden planks that stretched bank to bank, the gaps between them wide enough for a mouse to fall through. She chose one and scampered across safely. Reaching the far side, she hurried along the edge of Tar Road, which took her by the bottom of Bannock Hill.

As Lilly approached Gray House, she noticed the yellow bulldozer. It caused her to stop. Though she was relieved it hadn't moved, just seeing the huge machine squatting there, gross and ominous, made her heart beat quicken and her small, round ears begin to twitch ever so slightly. Then she turned toward Gray House and spied the red flag flying from the roof—her father's way of announcing an emergency. She ran the rest of the way to Gray House.

"Hey, Lilly," called one of her cousins as she hurried up to the dilapidated building. "Did you find Poppy?"

A grim Lilly didn't even answer.

"Lilly," called another. "Is Poppy coming?"

"Where's Poppy?"

"Did you find her?"

"Is Poppy going to come?"

Why do they always ask for Poppy? thought Lilly as she scrambled up the porch steps and into the house without replying. The great number of mice milling about the doorway made it hard to get far. "Excuse me!" she said, pushing her way through. "Can I get past? Sorry. Please!" She headed right behind the front hall steps. There Lungwort had established his private study in an old boot that Farmer Lamout—the original human owner of the farm—had left behind years ago.

The boot was comfortably lined with odd bits of potato sacking. A couple of windows—covered with napkin bits—had been chewed through the leather. An old plaid necktie curtained the entryway.

Out of respect for Lungwort's position as head of the family—and now for his age and infirmities—no one entered the boot without permission of Sweet Cicely, Lungwort's wife and Lilly and Poppy's mother. As far as Lilly knew, Lungwort's boot was just about the only truly private place remaining in Gray House.

When Lilly finally reached the boot, she halted and

caught her breath. Once composed, she pulled the curtain aside and called softly, "Mama? Are you there, Mama? It's me, Lilly. I'm back!"

Sweet Cicely stepped out of the boot. She was small even for a deer mouse, with soft, pale-gray eyes, thin whiskers, and a nervous habit of flicking her ears with her paws as if they were dusty. Her orange-brown fur was flecked with white.

"Oh, Lilly," she said. "I'm so glad you got back. Papa will be much relieved."

"How is he?" asked Lilly.

"Very much the same," said Sweet Cicely. "Troubled and full of complaints as always, the poor dear." She looked about and gave her ears a quick, nervous flick. "But Lilly, dear, where's Poppy? Were you not able to find her? Isn't she coming?"

"Oh no, I'm afraid she is coming."

Sweet Cicely blinked. "*Afraid* she's coming? But why?"

"Mama, Poppy has, well . . . she's become . . . different."

Sweet Cicely put a paw before her mouth in alarm. "Good gracious! Different in what way?"

"She lives in a dead tree. Has a husband. And eleven unruly children. "

"Oh my."

"She's not nearly as refined as she used to be. Or gracious.

The truth is, Mama, she's become quite . . . insensitive."

Sweet Cicely sighed. "It was after that Ragweed got into her life that she changed. She became—"

Lilly finished the sentence: "Coarse."

"Ragweed *was* a difficult sort," said Sweet Cicely. "Not a good influence. Always demanding answers to everything. And then, to die so young, so tragically. You know, I was— of course I was—dreadfully sorry about his death." Sweet Cicely lowered her eyes for a respectful moment. "But then, Lilly, as you also know perfectly well, that mouse would simply not listen to your papa. What happened was Ragweed's own fault. But surely Poppy isn't that way . . . is she?"

"Mama, she married Ragweed's brother."

"Did she!"

"He's a golden mouse, too."

"Golden!"

"Then, Mama, Poppy named one of her children . . . Ragweed."

Sweet Cicely gasped.

"And Mama—she's bringing that young Ragweed here."

"Here?"

Lilly nodded.

"But—" Sweet Cicely flicked her ears nervously.

"It's terrible to say so about your grandchild," said Lilly, "but this new Ragweed is, well, not so very different from his namesake. To begin, he's dyed himself completely . . . black."

"Black!"

"With a white stripe down his back."

"Merciful mercy!"

"He's very rude. And he—they call him Junior, by the way—is bringing a friend. . . ."

"Heavens to betsy!" cried Sweet Cicely. "What a time to bring a friend."

"This friend, Mama"—Lilly had become quite shrill—"is . . . a . . . *skunk!*"

Sweet Cicely patted a paw over her mouth.

"Mama," Lilly confided in a lower voice, "it was all I

could do to get Poppy not to bring a horrid porcupine friend of hers along."

"Lilly, do you mean to say those rumors we heard, that Poppy had a good friend who is a . . . porcupine, were true?"

"I told you they weren't rumors, didn't I? And if ever there was an unpleasant, gross, offensive . . ."

Sweet Cicely's whiskers drooped. Her tail whipped about. With each word her voice went up. "Is Poppy bringing that . . . porcupine here?"

"No, no," said Lilly. "But only because I put my paw down."

"Oh, please, Lilly," said Sweet Cicely. "You mustn't even whisper the word 'porcupine' in the presence of your papa. You know how he still is obsessed about them."

"Is that you, Lilly?" called a rather feeble voice from within the boot.

"Yes, Papa," called Lilly. "I'm right here."

"Why are you wasting your time out there with your mother? You should be talking to me!"

Mother and daughter exchanged sympathetic, knowing looks. "You'd best go in," whispered Sweet Cicely. "I'll be fine." She held back the cloth that covered the entryway and whispered, "Lilly, dear, please, please, be careful what you tell him."

"You don't wish me to fib, do you?"

"No. No. Of course not. But, as my mother used to always remind me, 'When in doubt, leave it out.'"

"But, Mama, I have no doubts," said Lilly. She held up her leaf packet of pine seeds. "I did bring Papa some seeds."

"Oh, Lilly, I do wish your father grasped what a good daughter *you* are."

Lilly smiled ruefully, gave her mother's paw a reassuring squeeze, and went through the plaid necktie.

CHAPTER 16

Lungwort

LILLY PASSED DEEP INTO THE BOOT. It was gloomy, the air suffused with the sour smell of old age and illness.

"Come along, Lilly!" called Lungwort. "Don't dawdle so."

Lilly found her father in the boot's toe, resting on a bed of matted milkweed. Though Lungwort had been rather stout, the old mouse had become much thinner of late. His fur was almost completely gray, his tail bony. Still, his whiskers, despite having also turned quite gray, were still elegantly curled. As for the ivory thimble that he had always worn as a cap of authority, it sat beside him.

As Lilly emerged from the gloom, Lungwort propped himself up on an elbow and looked around at her. She paused. It saddened Lilly to see how lackluster her father's face had become. Quite pinched, it made his front teeth, which had always protruded slightly, even more prominent. His eyes, moreover, had a new and disturbing tendency to shift in and out of focus. And he often coughed—a deep, hacking wheeze that seemed to shake him deeply.

"Did you find Poppy?" Lungwort asked immediately.

"Yes, Papa."

"You didn't meet any porcupines along the way, did you?"

"Well . . . no, Papa."

"If porcupines had their way, they would take over the world."

"I'm sure, Papa."

"And that bulldozer is still there. Humans brought it, but I suspect there's a porcupine behind it somehow. I presume you noticed I've had the red flag raised. Is Poppy coming?"

"Yes, Papa."

The old mouse went though a fit of coughing. "I hope she knows," he resumed, "that it's time for her to be a dutiful daughter and meet her responsibilities. To me. To the family. This business of going off elsewhere with someone or other always was absurd. Married, the rumor is, without my permission. Then there's that other rumor that she's befriended a porcupine. I don't believe that, of course, but even rumors can be disturbing. Doesn't she understand I've important plans for her?"

"What plans?" asked Lilly.

"That's for your sister's ears, not yours," said Lungwort after another brief coughing spasm. "But did you tell her all that?"

"Yes, Papa," said Lilly.

"Good. I'll explain everything to her privately, tell her just what she must do, provide good advice, point out the direction to go, and inform her about those upon whom she can rely. You're sure you told her all this?"

"Yes, Papa, most of it."

"Good. Good. Of course, I'll be able to say it better than you. Now Lilly, I've no more need for you. Feel free to gossip with your mother if you like, but do let me know the moment Poppy arrives. I can't wait to tell her what's in store for her."

"Can't you tell me?" asked Lilly.

"No. It's for Poppy's ears and hers alone." Lungwort wheezed again and fell back onto his bed.

"Is there anything else I can do for you?"

"Let me be in peace. Good-bye."

"Papa, I brought you some pine seeds." Lilly held out her full leaf.

"Fine. Fine. Just leave them and go."

Lilly, wiping away a tear, withdrew.

CHAPTER 17

Poppy's Return

WHEN POPPY DISCOVERED that Junior and Mephitis were not where she had left them, she was annoyed. First she thought they had simply wandered off. Only after considerable time had passed without their showing up did it occur to her that they might have gone ahead. The thought of those rude youngsters bursting upon the family without her being there to soften the way caused her considerable unease.

Then the notion came that they might have decided to return to the snag. Yes, it was what she had wanted, but Junior and Mephitis were much too young to be traveling alone through the forest.

Regardless, they should have told her what they were doing. "How inconsiderate!" she cried. "*Why* must Junior make so many problems?"

The next moment her frustration turned to anger. "Bother on him!" she said. "I can't wait about! If he's gone off, that's his problem! I hope he did go back to the snag."

With that, Poppy jumped into the creek and gave herself another scrubbing to get rid of any skunk stink remains. She reached the other side by wading and swimming, and then scrambled up the high bank, where she could see for some distance.

"Oh my," she exclaimed as she gazed upon the view that lay before her. There, in one great prospect were the Old Orchard, Gray House, Tar Road, and beyond, Bannock Hill. The setting of her entire early life—all there! With this sight came an unexpected rush of memories and emotions that had her giggling one moment—they had played hide-and-seek endlessly right *there*: Cousin Basil had been caught in some brambles *there*—while the next moment she was ready to burst into tears, for at the top of Bannock Hill was where her beloved first Ragweed had died.

Her strong emotions took her completely by surprise. *Oh, why*, she heard herself thinking, *did I stay away for so long?* The answer came just as quickly: *Because I'm not what I was— and they won't understand!*

Poppy had to sit down. "Think good thoughts," she urged herself. "It will be fun to visit. It will! Well," she added ruefully, "mostly."

Only after some moments had passed did Poppy notice that sitting off to one side of Gray House was a yellow bulldozer—huge and powerful. It was not moving but just *sitting* there. Lilly had told her that everyone was sure it was poised to crush the house. How horrifying! No wonder a red flag was flying from the roof. Where would the family go? *Thank goodness I have a safe place to live,* Poppy reminded herself.

Poppy knew she had lingered long enough. She had to get on. Taking a deep breath, she told herself to be brave—even as she wondered what in the world she needed to be brave about. It was her *own* old home, her own family she was visiting! Really! She stood up—*Why are my legs feeling so weak?*—and started for Gray House, her heart pounding hard. "Oh, you silly mouse!" Poppy cried out loud. "Stop this fool-ishness! It shouldn't take courage to visit your own family!"

Yet her next thought was *Oh, but it does.*

Even so, Poppy plunged in among the high grasses, which meant she momentarily lost sight of the house. Knowing the way as if she had last walked it a day ago, she pressed on. What Poppy did not know was that her path took her just a few feet from where Junior and Mephitis lay napping. She saw no sign of them.

Poppy had almost reached the end of the orchard when she came upon a cluster of lady's slippers. The flowers—delicate purple, pink, white, and blue—stirred gently in the calm afternoon sun, shedding the sweetest of perfumes.

Poppy gazed at them. She always had loved them so. How much she would have liked to share them with her family, but they could never grow in the dim light of the forest.

Suddenly Poppy felt a powerful longing for Rye—so steady, so kind, and so loving. And the children. How much she missed them! The next moment—Poppy was hardly aware of what she was doing—she pulled a flower down, plucked it, and began to dance. Her steps were slow and, because she was out of practice, not particularly graceful. But her old desire to dance to the vibrant music that filled her heart was as strong as ever. As she did, her mind flooded with the thought *Oh, I do love being alive!*

She stopped, abruptly. "Poppy!" she scolded herself. "You are being ridiculous! You are the mother of eleven!" With a self-deprecating snort, she tossed the flower away, only to regret her gesture. She ran to retrieve it and nuzzled the supple petals by way of asking forgiveness. Then she laid the flower down with humble reverence. "Silly mouse!" she said out loud, giggled, and gave herself a hug. Now she felt ready to face whatever lay ahead.

Gray House loomed before her. She stopped and considered it: it seemed smaller than she remembered and much more dilapidated, truly a wreck.

"Hello there!" came a voice.

Poppy started. For a moment she couldn't speak to the mouse who stood before her.

"May I be of some help—," began the other mouse. He gasped. "Good gracious," he cried. "It's *Poppy*! Don't you recognize me? It's Basil!"

"Basil!" screamed Poppy. And she threw her paws about her favorite cousin.

Then came a torrent of questions and statements, both of them talking simultaneously: "How are you—You look *so* good—I am *so* happy to see you—It's been so long—You don't know how often I've thought of you—Why have you never visited?—Are you happy?—No, no, it's you I want to know about! *I* am so glad to see you—You've hardly aged at all—Neither have you—You should have sent word— How is your family?—Tell me everything you've been doing—What's new?—What's old?—You must meet my wife—You must meet my husband—You look wonderful— Oh my, it's *so* exciting to see you!"

Who said what, or when, and what might have been answers, or questions, or statements, neither knew, neither cared, neither bothered to know, and besides, it did *not* really matter, not one bit, no, no, not at all! For when they had gone through all of that, they started right in again with the same questions, the same answers, only perhaps a little slower. And perhaps a few new answers were slipped in, though neither cared to explain much about their own lives in their rush to find out everything about the other. That accomplished, or at least partly accomplished, they hugged each other yet again and laughed and cried.

At last Poppy said, "Lilly came and told me things were not good here. That's why I came. Basil, is it really true?"

"Actually, life is pretty much as it was when you left," said Basil. "Except Lungwort is quite a bit older. Not his old self. We are very crowded. And then there's *that*." He nodded to the bulldozer.

"When will it happen?" asked Poppy.

"No one knows for certain," said Basil. "Probably soon. That makes us all jumpy. But we can talk about that later. Let's get to the house. We knew—or at least hoped—you were coming. Everybody is dying to see you."

Poppy grinned.

They hurried toward the house.

Now Poppy met first one relation and then another and another. Everywhere she was greeted with excitement and warmth, hugs and caring questions. "Hey, Poppy! So glad to see you! Where you been so long?" she heard over and over again. By the time she reached the steps to Gray House, so many well-wishers and greeters surrounded her, it was hard to keep going. In the midst of it all Poppy, feeling so very happy, could hear herself thinking, *Why was I ever worried?*

Then she looked up. There was Sweet Cicely. She was standing right next to Lungwort—supporting him, really. *Oh my!* The two *had* aged a good deal. But, as always, her father had his thimble cap on his head. He was looking very stern, and he was saying: "There you are, Poppy. What's taken you so long, mouse? Come along now. There are urgent things to decide!"

In an instant it was exactly as it had been before: her stern, pompous father, telling her, a rather timid little mouse, what to do. Lungwort spoke as if time had not passed, as if life had not changed. *But it has,* thought Poppy as she started forward. *It has!*

CHAPTER 18

Poppy and Lungwort

THE CROWD QUIETED. A clear pathway was opened. Poppy felt her paw squeezed, and Basil's voice came in her ear: "You can handle it."

Poppy barely had time to nod before climbing the steps. She gave her mother a hug—or at least started to. Sweet Cicely held her daughter away and wrinkled her nose. "Poppy, dear," she said, "you're older!" It sounded like an accusation.

Before Sweet Cicely could speak another word, Poppy heard Lungwort say, "Come, come, Poppy. Don't dawdle." He grabbed her paw even as he coughed. "You and I have vital things to discuss."

Poppy let herself be pulled into the house. Lilly was there, frowning. Poppy smiled weakly at her, tried to hold back again, but her father led her away. Not even Sweet Cicely was allowed to come along.

As Poppy went with Lungwort, she looked about in

astonishment: Gray House was not the way she recalled it. It was so much more crowded. Mice were milling about like a parade that had nowhere to go. A beehive had more privacy. There hardly seemed room for living. With yelling the principal mode of communication, Poppy's ears rang with squeak and squeal as mice talked, argued, and chatted. The calm, still world of Dimwood Forest was as distant as the moon.

Within moments Poppy and Lungwort were deep in the old farmer's boot. After the bright sun, the noisy, warm reception by her family, and the chaos of the house, Poppy found the boot gloomy, stifling.

Lungwort had set his thimble cap down to one side and eased himself, with a slight cough, onto his milkweed bed. There he lay, panting and wheezing from his exertions. Poppy studied him. He *had* aged considerably. His face had thinned. His gaze was unsteady, his breath uneven. *He's fragile*, she thought. Even the ivory thimble lacked its normal polish. All the same she asked, "How are you, Papa?"

Lungwort batted the air with a paw as if it were an irritant. "Now Poppy, no need to waste time on chatter about foolish matters. I dislike chitchat. We're at a momentous point in the history of this illustrious family. One of those moments that have marked the past—and will no doubt mark the future—with a sense of profound history."

"Papa," said Poppy, "do you mean the possible destruction of Gray House?"

"Well, yes, there's that. Of course. But what I had in mind—in particular—was *your* future."

"Mine?" cried a startled Poppy.

"Don't interrupt. Just listen." Lungwort fussed with his whiskers. "Now then, your first order of business will be to rid us of the threat of that machine of destruction—the bulldozer."

"Papa," said Poppy, "I don't have any idea how to do that."

"Then you had best find one," said her father. "Secondly, you need find a solution for the overcrowding here."

"It does seem bad. What about the place I found near New House?"

"Never been there. I like it here. Anyway, I'm told it's become just as crowded. Besides, it's Gray House that should concern you. It's your ancestral home. So, finally, it's about time you assumed your role as the head of this great family, Poppy."

"Me! The head!"

"Yes, you. You are the one I'm appointing."

Poppy stared at her father in astonishment. Perhaps it was because she didn't want to think of what he had said, but the next moment she thought of something else: she had not seen Junior at Gray House. If he was not here, where could he be?

CHAPTER 19

Junior's Color

IN THE OLD ORCHARD Mephitis woke from his nap. Even so, he lay quietly beneath the warm late afternoon sun, enjoying his drowsiness and the sun-stroked warmth of his black fur. Only gradually did he allow himself to recall where he was and what he was doing: visiting Junior's family. That caused him to think of his own family, but when he did, his feelings of pleasure faded, replaced by melancholy.

He looked about for Junior. When the skunk realized Junior was no longer leaning against him, he became alarmed. Sitting up on his rear legs, he looked about. His best friend was walking toward a bush. "Hey, where you going?" Mephitis called.

"That blackberry bush," said Junior. "I can use the berries to make myself black again. That way, when I tell my mother's family that we're brothers, at least we'll look it."

"That's cool," said the skunk, pleased by the idea.

Using his tail to balance himself, Junior stood on his rear legs
to pluck a large, ripe berry. "Come
here!" he shouted. Mephitis waddled over. "Squeeze the berry
down over me," Junior proposed.

Mephitis took the black-
berry and smashed it between
his front paws. When the juice ran
down, Junior rubbed it deep into
his fur. They repeated this a few times.

"How do I look?" Junior finally said, stepping back
from the skunk.

"Well . . . freaking weird."

"How come?"

"Mouse, you're all . . . red."

"Red!"

"Like a radish."

Junior looked down
at himself, back and
front. "How come
they call them *black-*
berries?" he asked.

"Don't ask me," said Mephitis. "I didn't name the things."

"Maybe I should go to the creek and wash off."

"Suit yourself," said Mephitis. "But I bet there aren't a lot of red mice in the world. Know what I mean? Really sick."

Junior grinned. "Oh wow! Do I look like I've been dipped in . . . blood?"

Mephitis grinned. "Yeah, right."

"Nasty!" exclaimed Junior. "That'll spin their eyeballs. Skunk, they're going to really hate us now."

"I guess," said Mephitis, not quite so enthusiastic.

"Yeah. I'm pumped," said Junior. "Let's go."

Side by side, they walked through the orchard. Neither spoke, though occasionally Junior looked down at his fur. Gray House loomed larger and larger.

"Mouse," said the skunk, coming to an abrupt halt. "I've been thinking: maybe you should go on first."

"Alone?" cried Junior in alarm.

"Sure. That way you could see what's going down. I can wait here. Then, if everything is okay, you come and get me. Look, your Aunt Lilly doesn't even want me to come. Probably true for all the others, too. Check it out. I don't mind waiting."

"Hey, homie, we're supposed to be doing this *together*."

"We can. Only later."

Junior turned from his friend and looked at the house.

The silence was prolonged. "Hey, Mephitis, want to know something?"

"What?"

"I don't want to go, either."

"You turning chicken?" asked Mephitis.

"I'm a mouse, dude."

"I thought a mouse has to do what a mouse has to do," said the skunk.

"Well, I wish my mother never asked me to come."

"Yeah, but she did, and you did, so now you're done," said the skunk. "Anyway, your mother will be worried."

"How come you're so nervous about my mother all the time?"

"It's not all the time. Anyway, I like her."

"Yo, skunk," said Junior. "She's just a mother. Big deal. Let me tell you, nothing special about my mother." He stared at the house. "But if I do go ahead, you're going to stay right here, right?"

"Yeah."

"Promise?"

"I said I would, didn't I?"

"Okay," said Junior. "I'll be back fast as I can."

"Don't worry about me," said Mephitis, but when Junior didn't move, he said, "What's the matter?"

"I'm seriously sorry I came," said Junior.

"But you have to. It's your family."

"How come you always talk about *my* family?" said Junior. "What about yours?"

Mephitis shrugged. "Mom and Dad got sick. Died."

"Oh," said Junior, suddenly afraid to look at his friend. "Brothers? Sisters?"

"Just me."

"I thought you said—"

Mephitis shrugged again.

"Ever wish you had parents around again?" said Junior.

"Too late for that," said Mephitis, looking down.

Junior felt he should say something more, but was fear-

ful of using the wrong words. "Hey, what I was saying about mothers—"

"Forget it."

"Okay," said Junior.

For a moment neither spoke.

"Just make sure," said Junior, "you wait here."

"Right."

Embarrassed to think that he had made a fool of himself, and perhaps a little angry that Mephitis had allowed him to do so, Junior wanted to get away. He started for Gray House. "Smell you later," he said.

"Yeah," said Mephitis, and watched his friend go, the bright red fur easy to follow in the green grass. Once, twice, Junior turned and looked back. The last time he waved.

As soon as Mephitis was sure Junior was not going to look back any more, he turned in the opposite direction. "No point hanging around," said the skunk. "Hey, except for maybe Junior, nobody likes me. Not really." Tears stung his eyes. "Mephitis," he told himself. "Face it. Why would anybody like a skunk? Why don't you do the world a favor and go jump in the river?" With that he put his pointy black nose to the ground and waddled off in the direction of Glitter Creek.

CHAPTER 20

A Red Mouse at Gray House

It was a nervous junior who made his way out of the Old Orchard toward Gray House. Disappointed that his friend had not come along with him, he paused twice to glance back. The first time he looked, he could still see Mephitis, his black-and-white tail wagging in the grass. The second time he looked, the tail was gone. Junior stood and stared. "Probably went back to sleep," he muttered, wishing he were doing exactly that.

Junior sighed. He was sorry he had asked Mephitis about his parents. He had had no idea the skunk's parents were dead. He hoped Mephitis wasn't mad at him for asking. He looked down at himself. He was very red. *Maybe*, he thought, *being bloody looking is* not *such a good thing.* He rubbed his belly. Though his paws turned pinker than normal, his belly didn't change at all. Junior flung himself down and rolled about in the grass. He remained red.

Mama is going to kill me, Junior thought with increasing nervousness. Next moment he decided his predicament was not his fault. If Poppy hadn't invited him, he would never have come to Gray House. *It's all so dumb* was the phrase that kept running through his head. *And if they see me with Mama*, he thought as he continued on, *they'll think I'm still a baby.*

Junior moved forward, only to pause and look back one more time. Still seeing no sign of Mephitis, the mouse pressed forward, eyes down, staring at his feet. When he finally did look to check his path, there stood another mouse directly in front of him. What's more, the mouse was staring openmouthed at Junior.

Junior came to a halt. *Uh-oh, Mama's family. I think I'm gonna puke,* he thought.

Junior cast his eyes down and crouched close to the ground. He told himself to hide all emotions: *the less I show them*, he thought, *the more invisible I'll be.* Even so, he stole a look at the staring mouse and saw then that the mouse was young—younger than he. Junior felt better.

"Hey, hello!" called the young mouse.

"Hello yourself," returned Junior.

"Who . . . and . . . what are you?" the young mouse asked. He was staring wide-eyed at Junior.

Junior frowned. "I'm a mouse," he muttered. "What do

you think?" He belched, only to be immediately sorry he had. What was always so funny with Mephitis now felt dumb.

"I sort of guessed you were a mouse," returned the youngster. "But I never saw a red mouse before. What kind of mouse are you? Or are you just wounded?"

"I'm a golden deer mouse. That okay with you?"

"Oh, sure. It's great. No problem. Where do you come from?"

Junior waved in the direction of the forest.

"The forest?"

"Yeah."

"Dimwood Forest?"

"Right."

"Wow. That's amazing. How come you're here?"

"My old mouse used to live around here."

"Your mother?"

"Yeah."

"What's her name?"

"Ah . . . Poppy."

"*Poppy?*" shrieked the young mouse.

"You have some problem with that?" said a scowling Junior as he reared up on his hind legs and balled his paws into fists.

"You saying your mother is . . . Poppy? *The* Poppy?"

"What's the big deal? Do you know her?"

"Know her? Of course I know her. Everyone knows

Poppy. She's famous."

"She is?"

"Hey, duh, think of all the things she's done."

"What do you mean?"

"Oh, come on. For one thing, she fought Mr. Ocax."

"Who's he?"

"You sure Poppy's your mother? I mean, you must be joking. You gotta know, Mr. Ocax, the owl. The one who was dictator over this whole area."

"Oh . . . yeah," said Junior, who had never heard the

name before. "That one."

"You gotta know how, all alone, your mother dueled him—one porcupine quill against all his talons and beak. And she won! That owl got killed. So we were all free. Then she found this whole other place for the family to live. New House. And she had this friend, a giant porcupine. Then she went off to have more adventures in the forest. With beavers and stuff. I mean, she must be the most famous mouse in the whole world! And you're her son? That's fantastic. Cool. Like, you're not just kidding me?"

"Why should I?"

"Well, if *you* don't know . . . But that's amazing. You are so lucky! I wouldn't think with all her adventures she'd have time to have kids! What's your name?"

"Junior."

The young mouse held out his paw. "How do you do, Junior. My name is Cranberry. I'm really glad to meet you. I mean, seriously honored. Yow, Poppy's son! That's so amazing! No one is going to believe that I met you first. But I did, didn't I? I'm so lucky. Maybe not as lucky as you, but you better come on. All my friends will give pips to meet you. I mean, your mother, I mean, she . . . must be the coolest mother in the whole world!" The young mouse started to run toward Gray House, only to stop and cry, "Come on!"

Junior, hardly knowing what to make of what he had

heard, followed along at a slower pace, which meant the other mouse kept waiting for him to catch up. As they drew closer to the house, Junior began to see other mice.

"Hey, you guys," yelled Cranberry. "Guess who I found? It's Poppy's son! No, really! Her real son! His name is Junior. And I met him first."

Within moments a ring of staring young mice surrounded Junior. They gazed at him, pink noses sniffing, whiskers quivering.

"He lives in the forest," Cranberry explained with excited authority. "He's a golden deer mouse, but as you can see, he's all red."

"Is Poppy really your mother?" one of the other mice found the courage to ask.

"I guess," said Junior, eyes cast down toward the ground.

"Is it true she's amazingly strong?"

"I don't—"

"Sure she is," one of the other mice answered. "Everyone knows she kills owls and other huge, mouse-eating birds. And she's a genius, too." She turned to Junior. "Right?"

Junior said, "Well, maybe, but—"

"It's so true," said another mouse. "The whole universe knows she's had these amazing adventures. How could you not know it? Wow! It would be so fantastic to have a mother who did those things. Isn't that right?" he asked Junior.

"I suppose."

"Doesn't she talk about all that stuff?"

"No."

The mice stared in disbelief at Junior.

"Whaddya mean?" someone finally said.

Junior shrugged. "She just doesn't. That okay with you?"

Then another mouse said, "But you do know about all the things she's done, don't you?"

Junior felt his cheeks grow warm. "Sure. Sort of."

"You're just being modest," said another.

"Is it hard having a famous mother?"

"Not really."

"Can you tell us something she did? Something no one knows about?" The other mice quickly joined in, creating a chorus. "Please tell us! We won't tell anyone. We promise."

Junior looked around. The mice were waiting for him to say something. "Well," he said, "on the way over here, we were attacked by a bear."

"A bear!" they cried in horrified unison.

"But," Junior continued, "she got us away."

"That's just what Poppy would do," said one of the mice. "So amazing. A bear. How did she *do* that?"

"A friend—a skunk."

"She has a friend who's a skunk?" cried a mouse.

"Yeah. She called him and he—and I—helped."

"You did?"

"I'm cool."

"That's incredible!"

"I've heard one of your mother's best friends is a monster porcupine," said another. "Is that true?"

"Yeah."

There were ooohs and ahs.

"That's so cool," one of mice said. "Lungwort—he's head mouse here—he says we should always stay away from porcupines. What's Poppy's friend like? Is he scary? Do you like him? Do you ever see him?"

"Uh, sure."

"What's his name?"

"Ereth."

"He your friend, too?"

"He lives next to us."

The mice stared at him with awe.

"Did Poppy come to stay?" a mouse asked.

"She will," said another. "I'm sure she will."

"She's talking to Lungwort right now," said another. "Probably telling him what she's going to do about the bulldozer."

"Be easy for her."

"Wish my mother was like Poppy," said another mouse.

"Actually, I'm related to her. My father is her second cousin. I think."

"Lucky."

"I guess," said Junior, "I better go find her."

"We'll take you," called someone. "But hey, how come you're all red?"

"I . . . like it."

"It's so nasty. How'd you do it?"

"Blackberry juice."

"Wow! That's what I'm going to do, too."

"Me, too."

"No, me!"

Junior, swept along by the crowd of mice, looked up. Gray House was just ahead of them. It seemed huge, ungainly. Ugly. But even more than that, he could see his mother on the porch, and she was looking right at him. She did not look happy.

CHAPTER 21

Mephitis Meets Someone

A DEJECTED MEPHITIS WADDLED slowly through the Old Orchard in the direction of Glitter Creek. He was very sorry he had come on this trip. It had nothing to do with Junior. Junior was his best friend. For that matter, his only friend. It was just that he had thought the trip would be fun. Something different. But all the talk of Junior's family upset him. It reminded Mephitis of his own family—the one he didn't have. He had never felt lonelier.

That the day was bright and balmy was nothing to him. That he kept brushing by bright flowers, passing by fallen, crisp, ripe apples, was of no importance. He hardly felt or smelled the tall, sweet grasses that brushed his face. He would have preferred a soggy, gloomy rain. If it rained, he would have an excuse to dig under a rock or curl up in a log and go to sleep. Better to sleep than to be lonely.

Sleep passed the empty times. Sleeping meant he didn't have to solve problems. And if he didn't try to solve problems, he couldn't fail at it. He hated failing. Best of all, if he slept, he didn't have to think. He had done a lot of napping before he became friends with Junior.

Except—Mephitis was not sleepy.

He did feel badly that he had broken his promise to Junior about staying at Gray House. But if the mice there were like Junior's Aunt Lilly, endlessly complaining about his stink and his manners, it would just be awful. Skunks stunk, sometimes. That's the way it was. A good thing, too. He had chased the bears away, hadn't he?

Upon reaching the edge of the orchard, Mephitis had to decide which direction to go. What he really wanted was to run off to someplace where no one knew him. A new place. A place where he could be a brand-new skunk. Exactly how that skunk would be new and different, he wasn't sure. Maybe, if he went far enough away, it would be easier to figure out.

That thought led to another: he would go to the creek and follow it for as long as he could. He'd let the creek lead him.

His decision filled Mephitis with new energy. He hurried along and soon reached the bank of the creek, which he scrambled down so fast, he could hardly stop himself.

Except—someone was already there.

"Watch it, stink tail," said the porcupine. "You almost ran into me. That wouldn't be too smart."

When Mephitis realized it was the porcupine who lived near Junior's place, he backed away. "Sorry," he muttered. "Didn't see you."

"Try opening your eyes," muttered Ereth.

"I said I'm sorry," said the skunk. He wheeled about and started off down the side of the creek.

"Hold it!" cried Ereth.

Mephitis stopped.

"You aren't, by any crumb-covered chance, Junior's skunk friend, are you?"

"What if I was?"

"Then what are you doing here? Weren't you going with Poppy? Where is she?"

"Junior went to that mouse family house. I don't know where Miss Poppy is."

"How come you're not with them?" said Ereth.

"Changed my mind."

"Glad you have a mind to change," said Ereth.

"Buzz you," said the skunk, and started off again.

"Hey, whisper wit," cried Ereth. "Did you get into a fight with Poppy?"

Mephitis stopped. "No way."

"You rude to her? She send you home?"

"Why should I be nasty to her?"

"Because you're a teenager, snot soup."

"Hey, what is it with you?" said Mephitis. "How come you're always saying mean things? I'd never be rude to Miss Poppy. I like her."

"You do?"

"Yeah, she treats me decent, not like some I could mention."

"She treats everyone nice," muttered Ereth.

"Even you?" asked Mephitis.

"'Specially me," said Ereth.

"That's a stretch."

"Hey, blot brain, are you looking to get a prickly tail in your face?" Ereth advanced on the skunk.

"Get any closer, pincushion," returned Mephitis, "and you'll get some stink in your snout." He spun about, stood on his front paws, and aimed his backside right at Ereth.

"Snake suspenders!" cried Ereth, retreating a few steps. "Don't get yourself in an uproar. I was just worried about Poppy."

Mephitis lowered himself and took a few steps away, but then paused and looked around at Ereth. "The thing is," he said, "we got separated from Miss Poppy."

"How come?"

"Me and Junior went ahead. Figured she'd catch up to

us. But then Junior went on his own."

"How come you didn't go with him?"

Mephitis looked away. "I don't belong there. I mean, it's just for mice. Anyway, that Aunt Lilly didn't like me."

"And you let that bother you?"

"I guess."

"She didn't like me, either," said Ereth.

"You're right. She didn't."

"What did she say?"

"Said you were 'big and ungainly.'" Mephitis pursed his lips and folded his paws together as he repeated Lilly's words in his best imitation of her dainty speech.

"That mouse," said Ereth, "has as much brains as the pointy end of a sharp pin. What did Poppy say?"

"Told Lilly you were her best friend."

"Which is why," said the porcupine, "I thought I'd hang around in case she needed me."

"Know what? I chased a bear away from her."

"How'd you manage that?"

"My stink."

"Good for you!" cried Ereth. "A little stink in the right place can make the world sweeter."

"You really think so?"

"Hey, would you like things to be all one color?"

"No."

"Okay, then: what stinks up my nose could be sweet up yours."

Mephitis grinned. "Do you think I should stay around, too?" he asked.

Ereth stared at the skunk. "Suffering spider slippers. Between my quills and your stench, there isn't much the two of us couldn't chase off."

Mephitis laughed. "That's cool."

"Except I think we should get a little closer to that Gray House. Keep an eye on things."

"You mean me—with you?" said Mephitis.

"Depends how choosy you are about friends," said Ereth.

"Junior is always talking about you. About the things you say and do. Would you talk to me like that?"

"Dolphin dandruff! There's nothing special about the way I talk. I'll talk to you the way I talk to everybody. What's your name, anyway?"

"Mephitis."

"Okay, Misfit, let's go."

"Yes, sir."

"Not 'sir.' The name is Ereth."

Mephitis grinned, as side by side the skunk and the porcupine started back toward Gray House. As they went, Ereth talked and Mephitis listened.

CHAPTER 22

Poppy at Gray House

Poppy, standing next to Lungwort on the front porch, with Sweet Cicely and Lilly close behind, looked out over the milling crowd of mice. Wishing she knew where Junior was, Poppy made a movement to leave the porch, only to be restrained by Lungwort.

"I need to make a speech," said Lungwort, "and you need to be here."

"What sort of speech?" said Poppy.

"I'm going to announce that you are about to become the new leader of our family."

"Papa, please! I never said I would. I don't want to be. I don't live here. I have a family elsewhere. I'm going back home soon."

"Nonsense," said Lungwort. "We'll work out the details later. I need to inform everybody that you're going to deal with the bulldozer."

"Papa! I told you: I don't know what to do."

Lilly, who was standing right behind her, whispered, "Poppy, please don't argue with him. He'll only get upset."

"It will upset me a lot more," returned Poppy.

"Poppy," Sweet Cicely added, "you know your papa always does what's best for everyone."

"But—"

"Can't you," said Lilly, "show a little respect?"

Poppy tried to remember where she had heard that phrase before. But mice were now clustered all around and on the porch, and she did not want to argue in front of them, so she stayed put.

Lungwort went toward his regular speech-making place, an old straw hat. He tried to climb it on his own but found the going difficult. It was Lilly and Sweet Cicely who rushed forward. Pushing from below, they helped the old mouse ease into the hat's crown. Once there, Lungwort coughed twice, tapped his thimble cap down over his head—pushing his ears out a little more, cleared his throat, stroked his whiskers, and began.

"My fellow mice, as I strive to maintain our superior style of life, while resisting change, you know I always have your best interests at heart. Alas, we Gray House mice are now facing a grave crisis, indicated by the presence of yonder yellow machine of mass destruction. We are all in imminent danger.

"Having, however, considered all aspects of the problem, I have decided to let my daughter Poppy solve the problem. You are aware, I'm sure, of Poppy's many talents and achievements. In this she is certainly my daughter. Still, I can assure you I will not—of course—entirely withdraw into retirement, but shall provide Poppy with excellent advice and suggestions, etcetera, etcetera, based upon my many years of experience, so she will be enabled to do the hard job."

There were cheers from the mice as well as cries of "Thank goodness!" "It's about time!" "Change is what we need!" "Hurrah for Poppy!"

Lungwort held up a paw to still the crowd. "Now," he resumed after a bit of wheeze, "once Poppy has accomplished this immediate task, making our happy family home safe again, I will take the opportunity to retire into my boot's toe and let Poppy assume the thimble of family leadership, which I have worn with such humble dignity."

As a murmur of approval went through the crowd, Lungwort held up a paw. "No, no," the old mouse went on, "a little change is inevitable. But only a little. Now then, in days to come Poppy may well call upon you for assistance. I hereby request that you not stint in your support of her. Very well, I shall now ask Poppy to say a few words."

Poppy, blushing, stepped forward.

"Hurrah for Poppy!" someone cried out. That was followed by lots of others shouting much the same thing.

Poppy felt like an imposter. She did not plan to become head of the family And she truly didn't know what to do about the bulldozer. While she was happy, despite the current confusion, that she had come to visit, she certainly had no intention of staying. And right now she needed to get to Junior.

Even so, she took another moment to look out at the upturned faces, the pink noses, bright eyes, delicate whiskers, and large ears of her family. Gradually she noticed that one of the mice standing before her had bright red fur. Never before having seen such an oddly colored mouse, she stared. Perhaps the poor creature had a disease. Then she gasped: *it was Junior!* He was grinning. Then the thought came: *he's going to belch!*

"Hooray for Poppy," a small voice called, jarring Poppy back to her senses. She was just standing there, and all the mice still waited for her to say something.

"Thank you all," she began. "It's very nice to come for a visit. I'm afraid my father exaggerated when he listed all those things he wished me to do. But while I'm here, though my visit will be brief, I'll certainly try to be helpful.

"For the moment I just want to say hello to you all. That's my child over there," she said, pointing at Junior. "The . . . ah . . . red one. He's happy to be here, too."

All eyes turned to Junior. Not knowing where to turn, he did a half shrug, while offering up a shy smile.

"We both thank you," Poppy concluded.

There was a round of applause as Poppy came down off the steps. Ignoring her father's cries of "Poppy, we must confer right now!" she made her way through the crowd toward Junior.

As she passed among the mice, she was patted again and again, while a variety of mice called, "Thanks for coming, Poppy." "Sure great to have you back, Poppy." "We need you, Poppy." "You'll solve everything, Poppy."

Poppy, hearing the remarks, wondered if they would have so much confidence in her if they knew she couldn't keep track of the whereabouts—or the color—of her own son.

CHAPTER 23

Poppy and Junior

Yo, mama," said Junior, grinning as Poppy approached. He was gazing at her intently, trying to see in her the things he had been told she had done.

"Where did you two go?" said Poppy, not knowing whether she felt anger or relief. "Why didn't you tell me you were coming here? I was really worried."

"Sorry."

"And why are you all red?"

"Wanted to be."

Poppy looked around. "Where's Mephitis?"

"Waiting for me in the orchard."

As Poppy reminded herself that they were surrounded by mice, all of whom were looking and listening to their discussion, Junior grinned at her. "Hey, Mama," he said, "they really like you here. I heard some wild stories. Like about that owl, Mr. Ocax. Is that true?"

"I don't know what you've heard."

"How come you never told me about it?"

"I've been too busy, but—" She felt a tap from behind. She turned. It was Lilly.

"Papa says he really must talk to you," she said.

"I'll be right there," said Poppy. "Junior, come with me."

"But Mephitis—"

"He can wait. Now come!"

"Oh, all right."

Lilly led the way through the crowd with Poppy and Junior close behind. "No, really," Junior whispered, "*is* any of that stuff true?"

"This isn't the time to talk about it," said Poppy.

"This the house you used to live in?"

"Yes."

"It's stupid."

They climbed the porch steps and went into the house. Junior looked around. "Whoa, this place is so crowded," he whispered. "Everyone heaped together. Is it just huge rooms like this one?"

"There are six of them."

"Dumb," said Junior. "No place to be yourself."

"It wasn't so bad in the old days," said Poppy. She saw Sweet Cicely and moved toward her.

"Mama," said Poppy. "This is my son Ragweed Junior. Junior, this is my mother. Your grandmother."

To Poppy's surprise, Junior grinned, "'Lo, Mama's mama."

Sweet Cicely stared at the young mouse and then flicked her ears once, then twice. *"Ragweed?"* she said to Poppy. "Is that truly his name?"

"Yes, Mama."

"Oh dear. How . . . regrettable. And why . . . is he red? Is his father a red . . . mouse?"

Poppy turned to Ragweed. "Yes, Junior," she said. "Why in the world are you red?"

"The freaking berries weren't black."

"Freaking berries?" said Sweet Cicely, her brow furrowed. "What kind of berry is that?"

"I . . . got Mephitis to squeeze some over me."

"And his . . . odor?" asked Poppy's mother.

"Well . . . ," said Poppy. "He has a friend. . . ." Her voice trailed off, and for a moment no one said a word.

"My friend's a skunk," said Junior.

"A skunk?" echoed Sweet Cicely.

"Poppy," called Lilly from the entryway to the boot. "Papa is waiting. . . ."

"Perhaps," said Sweet Cicely, "Junior . . . might wait a bit."

"Why?" said Poppy.

Sweet Cecily flicked her ears. "Poppy, dear . . . his color . . . name . . . and smell. The other Ragweed was not one of your papa's favorites."

"Mama," said Poppy, "Junior's color is fine. As for his name, that's fine, too. Now he needs to meet his grandfather." She pushed Junior forward, and the two of them walked toward where Lilly was waiting.

"Hey, Mama," Junior said, "do you like my new color?"

"It's ridiculous."

"Hey, guess what? I never thought of you having a mama."

Poppy stopped. "Why?"

"That would mean you were . . . like me. That's too freaking weird."

"Maybe I am," said Poppy as she pulled the plaid tie away from the entry to the boot. "And if you could refrain from saying 'freaking' for the next five minutes, I'd very much appreciate it. Papa!" she called. "We're here!" She turned to Junior. "Come along."

"What's this place?"

"An old boot."

"What's a boot?"

"Never mind. Just brace yourself."

"For what?"

"Junior . . . just *freaking* brace yourself!"

Junior grinned and stayed close to his mother's side as they entered the dim boot and made their way to the toe.

CHAPTER 24

Lungwort Meets Junior

As POPPY AND JUNIOR APPROACHED, Lungwort sat up abruptly on his milkweed bed. He stared at Junior, eyes blinking rapidly, whiskers twitching.

"Papa," said Poppy, "this is your grandson."

Lungwort continued to gaze mutely at Junior. He coughed twice and then said, "My eyes must be getting much worse. This young mouse appears to be . . . red."

Poppy took a deep breath. "Papa he is red . . . for the moment."

"Who did you say he was?"

"Your grandson."

"My grandson?"

"Yo, old mouse," said Junior. "Are you Mama's papa?"

Poppy winced.

"I am," said Lungwort.

"That's frea—"

"Junior!" cried Poppy.

Junior squeezed his mouth shut with a paw.

Lungwort frowned. "Is his father red?"

"Rye," Poppy managed to say, "is a golden mouse."

"Why does this one smell?"

"Papa . . . he's a teenager."

Junior grinned.

Lungwort continued to stare at him. "I wasn't aware teenagers were required to smell. Does he have a name?"

Poppy hesitated for just a moment. Just as she was about to speak, Junior blurted: "It's Lungwort, dude. My name is Lungwort Junior. Only they always call me Junior." He held out a paw. "Pleased to meet you, old mouse. Mama always talks about you. Telling us what a cool mouse you are."

A startled Poppy stared at her son.

Lungwort beamed with pleasure. "My, my," he cried. "Named after me!" He turned to Poppy. "You never told me that." He took Junior's paw and pressed it warmly.

"But remember," Junior said, louder than before, "I only answer to Junior."

"Then Junior it is," chortled Lungwort. "I must say I am honored to be so memorialized."

"Now Papa—," Poppy began.

Lungwort cut her off with a raised paw. "Poppy, you

must leave me alone with this young mouse. He and I have much to say to each other."

"But—"

"Scoot, Mama," said Junior, grinning widely. "We Lungworts need to talk."

Poppy, with an imploring look at Junior, went out.

Left behind, Junior slapped Lungwort on the back. "Yo, Gramps, you're just the old mouse I need to talk to."

"About what, pray tell?"

"I need to know everything about my mama. All the bad stuff she did when she was my age. And that Ragweed she used to hang out with. What was up with him? The full load of dirt. And about you, too. I bet you were wild."

Lungwort laughed. "I think I can truly expound a fair amount about such subjects," he said. "Indeed, you and I do have much to talk about."

CHAPTER 25

Family Talk

Poppy, HER TAIL TWITCHING ever so slightly, made her way out of the boot. Lilly was waiting for her.

"Where's Junior?"

"He's with Papa."

"Alone?" gasped Lilly.

"They're getting on wonderfully."

"They are?"

"I think so." Poppy considered her sister. She seemed very tense, with eyes welling with tears. Her whiskers drooped. Her ears flicked forward and back. "Lilly, you look sad. What is it?"

Lilly shook her head.

After a moment Poppy said, "It's you who looks after Papa, isn't it?"

Lilly, wiping a tear from her cheek, nodded. "Well, Mama and I."

"And he takes it all for granted, doesn't he?"

When Lilly turned away, Poppy reached out and touched her sister. "Lilly, listen to me."

"You don't need to talk down to me," said Lilly, "just because you're the one who is going to become the head of the family."

"Lilly, how many times must I say it: I have no intention of doing that."

"But you will. I know you will. You get your way with things like that. You've always been Papa's favorite."

"Lilly, I was anything but his favorite. And I don't want to be head of this family. I am going back to *my* family."

"Why would you want to go back to that dark, dank forest and that dead tree with that dreadful, smelly porcupine living right next door?"

"And I," said Poppy, "can't believe you would want to live in a place without a shred of privacy."

Lilly held up her head. "I believe in loyalty to *my* family."

"Lilly, I'm loyal to mine," said Poppy with all the force she could muster.

"But how could you walk away from . . . all this?"

"Because my life has changed, Lilly. I like what it's become. I'm happy with it. Anyway, this house is about to fall down. For your sake, I hope it doesn't. But Junior is right: you're heaped together here. No privacy. Whatever happens, I am *not* going to stay."

"I still don't believe you," said Lilly, and she rushed off.

Poppy watched her go and started to follow, only to change her mind. The crowd of mice with all their noise had given her a headache. Hoping to find a quiet place, and tickled by a memory, she made her long way up to the attic of the house. Long ago, when no older than Junior, she had come upon a tin can shaped like a house, complete with chimney—which she used for an entryway. "Log Cabin Syrup," read the label. Poppy had licked the can clean, lined it with shreds of old newspapers, and declared it her private room. She was one of the few mice who wanted privacy. Moreover, Poppy suddenly recalled, she had liked it dark, like Junior among the snag's roots. Why had she done that? she asked herself. The answer came quickly: *That made it all my world.*

Upon reaching the attic, Poppy was disappointed to find it was as crowded as the rest of the house. Even so, she found her old can exactly where it had been and not looking very much different. She gave it a hard rap. It sounded as solid as ever. Heart swelling, she was just about to climb in when a sleepy young mouse, roused by the sound of Poppy's steps, popped up out of the chimney.

"Oh!" cried a startled Poppy. "I'm sorry. I didn't think anyone would be here."

"That's all right," said the sleepy mouse. "Who are you? Did you want me?"

"No . . . it's just . . . I . . . this used to be my own room."

The young mouse grew wide-eyed. "But—you're Poppy, aren't you?"

Poppy nodded.

"Was this *your* space?"

"Yes."

"I'm sorry," said the mouse, jumping up. "It was empty. But if you'd like—"

"No, no, that's all right," said Poppy, backing away in

haste. "It's not mine anymore. It's yours."

"Are you sure?"

"Yes."

"I'm . . . honored to have it," called the young mouse as Poppy hurried away.

Feeling annoyed to have found the young mouse in her old room, but even more annoyed that she *was* annoyed, a tear coursed down Poppy's cheek. "Silly mouse!" she scolded herself. "It's not your room! You left it a long time ago!" She sniffed, wiped the tear away, and then began to giggle. "Poppy, decide who you are!"

The main room was teeming with chattering mice. To escape the noise and chaos, Poppy went out to the back steps. It was just as crowded, but when the mice saw the newcomer was Poppy, they shyly withdrew. Poppy made no protest.

It was twilight. From the top of the back steps, Poppy could just see the edge of Dimwood Forest, like a distant curtain. Above it a half moon was rising. Thoughts of Rye and the children bedding down around the snag for the night filled her; she missed them terribly. Yet here she was at Gray House, quite convinced nothing could be done to save it.

"I wondered if you'd be out here," came a voice.

Poppy turned. It was her cousin Basil. "Can I join you?" he asked.

"Please," said Poppy. "I'm really glad to see you."

"Brought you some seeds," he said, offering Poppy a double paw of wheat berries.

"Thank you. I haven't eaten all day."

For a while the two sat side by side in silence, nibbling the seeds.

"Basil," said Poppy after a while, "have you noticed? When you're young, you don't want to be young. Then, when you're older, you don't want to be old. But I guess it doesn't matter what we want: we're always getting older."

"Oh my," said Basil, "you *are* low."

"A bit."

Neither of them spoke for a while, until Poppy said, "Thank you."

"For what? I haven't said anything."

"Exactly," said Poppy. "Among the many things I've learned to love about Dimwood are its silent moments. Silence fills me. I don't know how I ever lived here. It's so crowded. And noisy."

"Gray House certainly isn't quiet," agreed Basil. "With so many living here, there really is no privacy. Some of us think it might not be so bad if this old house did come down. We need a change. Problem is, no one knows how to bring it about."

"Basil," said Poppy, "everybody seems to think I can

come up with a way to deal with the bulldozer."

"You can't, can you?"

"I doubt it," said Poppy.

"We better do something before it happens," said Basil. "I don't think we have much time."

"Basil," said Poppy after a while, "why do you think our families are so hard?"

"Can't say."

"Maybe," said Poppy, "it's because they seem easy. It's like in the forest, where there are these game trails. It's much easier to follow one than to make a path of your own—but they don't always take you where you want to go, and after a while they vanish. And there you are . . . on your own anyway."

The two cousins spent most of the night talking quietly, catching up on family gossip: sisters, brothers, cousins, aunts, uncles, children, and spouses as well as shared friends. And when Basil finally left her, there were affectionate promises of more visits.

Finally a tired Poppy slept quite comfortably on the back steps. She didn't wake until she heard Lilly's voice cry, "Poppy! A human has just arrived! He's heading for the bulldozer!"

CHAPTER 26

The Derrida Deconstruction Co.

POPPY JUMPED UP. With Lilly by her side, she rushed through the deserted house. The porch was filled with mice peering through the lopsided pales of the porch fence. Others were on the steps, so densely packed, a few tumbled to the ground below. The squeaking and squealing was high pitched and shrill. All were staring in one direction, toward the old tar road. Poppy squeezed through and looked for herself. There, parked on the road, was a battered green pickup truck. But on the side door was a boldly lettered sign:

THE DERRIDA DECONSTRUCTION CO. AMPERVILLE

★ ★ ★

A man sat in the cab, staring at Gray House. As Poppy watched, he stepped out. He was a large man, with a large stomach, gray hair, and a withered face. He was wearing tan overalls, heavy work boots, and a peaked cap with the word *Amps* on it. For a while the man simply stood by his truck and gazed at Gray House. Then, after exchanging his cap for a yellow safety helmet and giving a hitch to his overalls, he walked slowly toward the bulldozer.

"He's going to knock the house down!" cried one of the mice.

There was a stampede to leave the porch.

"No! Wait!" cried Poppy. "Let's see what he does."

Breathless, the mice watched as the man went up to the bulldozer. He walked around it once, twice, occasionally tapping the treads with a boot. Then he climbed into the driver's seat.

"He's going to start it!" screamed a mouse.

"Be patient!" urged Poppy.

A few of the mice edged off the porch, but most stayed where they were.

A sleepy Junior appeared. "What's happening?" he asked.

"Come over here by me and watch," said Poppy.

The man in the bulldozer reached under the levers and seemed to turn something. There was a great roaring sound as the engine started. Black fumes bellowed from the exhaust pipe.

"Now!" Poppy commanded. "Off the porch! Empty the house! Leave your possessions. Just go!"

There was no holding the mice back. With a crescendo of terrified shrieking, they poured down the steps and tried to get away. Some of the mice were agile enough to leap from the porch. A few, pushed in the rush, fell. Happily none was hurt or trampled. Lungwort, supported on one side by Lilly and on the other side by Sweet Cicely, came, too, with Lilly calling, "Please make way for Lungwort! Let Lungwort through! Please!"

Poppy, with Junior by her side, remained where she was.

"Hey, Mama," Junior said, "don't you think we better move, too?"

"We've got a little time," said Poppy. "I can see what's happening better from here."

Junior glanced at his mother. Her calmness was a surprise to him. "You do like taking chances, don't you?" he said.

As the man continued to fuss over the machine, the great blade lifted and dropped, lifted and dropped.

"What's he doing?" Junior whispered.

"Shhh!"

With the blade up and more levers pushed, the motor roared louder than ever. Next moment the bulldozer jolted forward. The mice before the house began to flee.

The machine rumbled forward a few yards, turning first one way, then another, until it was aimed right at Gray House. Then, abruptly, it halted, blade up. The engine stilled. The man in the cab lifted himself out of the seat and stepped down to the ground. He began to walk toward the house.

"I don't get it," said Junior.

"Just watch," said Poppy. "But if he gets any closer, be ready to run."

A few yards from the house, the man stopped to survey the old structure, then continued on to the porch.

"Over here!" hissed Poppy. She ran to one side of the porch and hid behind a broken flowerpot. Junior stayed close.

The man stepped onto the porch, removed his yellow

helmet, and scratched his head. He looked through the
main door into the house and sniffed. Making a sour face,
he kicked the doorframe and gazed about. On the porch
he shook the old rail, causing it to fall off.

Slowly the man walked back to his truck. He took
one final look at the house, exchanged his helmet for his
peaked cap, and then climbed into the truck cab. In
moments he drove off.

The mice watched in deep silence.

"I don't get it," Junior whispered. "What did he do all that for?"

"I'm not sure," said Poppy, "Testing the machine, perhaps. I think he was deciding how best to knock the house down."

"When's he going to do that?"

"Soon, I suppose," said Poppy.

"I hate him," said Junior.

"Why?"

"It's our house, isn't it? Not his."

Poppy looked at him. "*Our* house?"

"What's wrong with saying that?" demanded Junior.

"I thought you hated it."

"I never said that."

The mice began to emerge from their hiding places and return to the house. Jabbering nervously to one another, they endlessly repeated what they had just seen, talking about what might happen next.

"Come on," Poppy said to Junior. "I'd like to look over the machine. Maybe we'll get some ideas. And I need to ask you a few things."

CHAPTER 27

Learning
Some Things

Junior, curious about the bulldozer, followed Poppy down the steps. The other mice, seeing the serious look on her face, said nothing, only made way so she could pass through.

"How did you get along with your grandfather?" Poppy said to Junior as they went along.

"He's wicked cool," said Junior.

"He is?"

"Yeah. When he was my age, he did all these crazy things."

"Like what?"

"He took this trip on a boat. And there was that time he joined up with traveling performing mice. He used to be an actor. How come you never told me about that stuff?"

"I didn't know about it," said Poppy.

"Why didn't he like my papa's brother—you know, Uncle Ragweed?"

"Ragweed often questioned things my father said."

"Why?"

"He didn't believe that just because my father said something, it was automatically true."

"What if I did that?"

Poppy stopped. "Junior, where's Mephitis? I feel responsible for him."

"Mama, you know what your problem is?"

Poppy sighed. "What?"

"You're a mama all the time. Why don't you just be yourself?"

"Just tell me about your friend."

"I think he got nervous about meeting the family. I told

him they would be nice, but he wanted me to come first. He's waiting for me out in the orchard. Hey! Guess what I found out? His parents died."

"Both of them?"

"Yeah."

"When?"

"Don't know."

"I'm so sorry. Why didn't you ever tell me?"

"I only just found out."

"Just?"

"Ma, he's my freaking best friend! You don't ask best friends personal stuff like that."

Poppy sighed. "Junior, how did you even get to be friends with Mephitis?"

Junior shrugged. "I don't know. Met him in the forest. He was all alone. Didn't have nobody, so I just thought . . . I don't know."

Poppy stared at Junior. "Are you saying you became friends to give him a family?"

"Well, yeah, sort of. I mean, what's the big deal? I like him. You got a problem with that?"

"Not at all," said a bewildered Poppy. "Not at all."

They walked on in silence. "Hey, Mama . . ."

"What?"

"You really are famous here."

"Am I?" Poppy said.

"Yeah. Gramps told me about you."

"He did?"

"I'm not sure he meant it that way, but actually, you were pretty cool. And lots of mice told me other neat stuff you did."

Poppy felt a swelling in her heart. "Do you think I'm cool?"

"Well, sure, a long time ago. Before you got old."

"Thank you."

"That's okay. But, all those adventures . . . You really do that stuff?"

"I suppose."

"How come you never told me?"

"You never asked."

"Everyone says you're going to be the head of the family—here."

"Never," said Poppy. They had reached the bulldozer. The two stared up at it and breathed in its cold smell of metal mixed with oil.

"It's huge," whispered Junior, his nose wiggling and sniffing.

Poppy went to one of the tracks. Reaching high, she pulled herself up and began to climb, her tail dangling.

"Where you going?" called Junior.

"Maybe I
can do something
to the engine."

"What's an engine?"
said Junior, following.

"It makes the bulldozer move."

"Hey," said Junior, "you do know a lot."

They reached the top of the treads and ran along them
until they reached the cab. With a leap, Poppy jumped

onto the cab floor. Junior followed. Once there, Poppy studied the big levers, the pedals, the key dangling from the dashboard. She knew, from watching the man, that each one probably had something to do with making the bulldozer go, but what did what, she had no idea.

"It's a monster," said Junior.

"Do you see any way to get into the engine?" said Poppy.

"Nope."

"Come on," said a disappointed Poppy. "We better

get back to the house."

"Mama, I need to find Mephitis."

"What are you going to do about your red fur?"

Junior grinned. "Actually, some of the young mice like it."

"And the smell?"

"Doesn't bother them. Gramps didn't care, either—after a while."

"Junior," said Poppy, "you do surprise me."

"Hey, you surprise me, too."

"Then we're even," said Poppy. "Better go find Mephitis. But Junior, when you come back, try and understand: my family probably doesn't know any skunks."

"Catch you later," said Junior. And with that, he bounded down to the ground and headed toward the Old Orchard. He had not gone far before he paused and looked back. "Mama!"

"What?"

"You may be old, but you're still pretty cool!"

Poppy watched him go. She shook her head. *Just when I think I understand him*, she thought, *he changes. Like everything else.*

She headed back to the house. As she went, she tried to think what she could possibly suggest to the family about the bulldozer and Gray House. The truth was, as she saw it, there was probably nothing they could do. Which meant Gray House was doomed.

CHAPTER 28

Junior and His New Friends

JUNIOR DID NOT GET VERY FAR before two young mice hailed him. "Hey, Poppy's son!"

Junior stopped. "The name's Junior, dude."

"Sorry. My name is Laurel. And this is Pine. You are Poppy's son, aren't you?"

"Yeah. What's up?"

"You probably don't remember, but when you first came, I was in that group who met you. That was so cool."

"Oh, sure," said Junior, though he did not remember.

"The thing is," said Pine, "can . . . can we ask you about your color?"

"And the way you smell," added Laurel.

"It bothering you or something?"

"Oh no! We think it's fantastic. You wouldn't believe how dull most mice are around here. Everybody looks and smells just the same."

"Yeah, well," said Junior, "where I come from, red is wicked."

The two mice exchanged quick glances.

"Is that really true?" asked Pine.

"Yeah," said Junior. "Anyone nasty works it that way. If you're with it, that is." Trying to keep from grinning, he said, "We call it 'Doing the stinky red.'"

"'Doing the stinky red,'" echoed Laurel, smiling broadly. "Do you think, you know, we could do the stinky red, too?"

"And look like me?" said Junior.

"Didn't you just say it's what everybody nasty is doing?"

"Yeah."

"Then that's what we want to do, too."

Junior held up his front paws. The mice slapped them. "Just come with me," he said, and raced off.

With Junior leading the way, the trio went into the Old Orchard. But when they reached the place where Junior was sure he had left Mephitis, his friend was gone.

"Is something the matter?" asked Pine.

"My friend was supposed to be here."

"Another mouse?"

"A skunk."

"Oh wow! Is he red, too?" asked Pine.

"Black. White stripe down his back. Bushy tail. Lays

down a stink like nobody's business."

"Is that the way you got your smell?" said Laurel.

"Sure."

"Do you think he would be willing to give us some?" said Pine.

"He'd love it. Mephitis!" Junior called. "You around?"

There was no reply. Junior's tail thrashed. He stroked his whiskers the way his father did.

"Are you worried about him?" asked Pine.

"Naw," said Junior. "Mephitis can freaking well take care of himself. You'll see, he'll be back soon. While we're waiting, I can show you how to dye your fur."

"Oh wow!"

Junior led his two new friends to the blackberry bush. "It's these berries," he explained. "My friend—who's a lot bigger than me—squished the berries over me. Turned me red fast."

"Maybe we could manage it," suggested Laurel.

"Give it a shot," said Junior as he searched about, then found a large blackberry and plucked it. He and Laurel held it over Pine's head, and together they squeezed. The red juice ran down. Laughing, the young mouse rubbed it over his fur. In moments he was mostly red, very much like Junior. A second berry completed the transformation.

"My turn," called a gleeful Laurel.

Junior and Pine repeated the process.

"How do we look?" said Pine.

"Wicked nasty," said Junior.

"I bet this starts a whole new style at Gray House," suggested Laurel. "Doing the stinky red."

"Only thing is," Pine pointed out, "we still need the smell."

"Have to wait for my friend," said Junior.

"Why don't you climb the tree and search for him?" suggested Laurel.

"Cool!" Junior found a low-hanging branch, grabbed

hold of its end and, with rear legs dangling, hauled himself up. Then he moved, slothlike, upside down along the branch. Upon reaching a thicker part of the branch, he swung topside and began to run along it. At the tree trunk he moved higher, then out again along a thick branch. At the farthest end he was able to look out over most of the orchard. First he gazed in the direction of Gray House, and then toward Glitter Creek. Finally he looked east, where Tar Road curved. Amid the tall grasses he spied Mephitis's tail moving along like a floppy black-and-white striped flag.

Junior sped down the tree trunk.

"Did you see him?" said Pine.

"Follow me!" cried Junior as he raced away. Every now and then he paused to call, "Hey, Mephitis! Wait up!"

The other mice stayed close.

At last Junior received a returning "Yo!" to his call. Plunging forward, he burst upon his friend. To his surprise, Ereth was at Mephitis's side.

"Hey," said Junior, "I thought you were going to wait for me over there."

"Got tired of waiting," said Mephitis.

"Oh." Junior looked at Ereth. "What are you doing here?"

"I go where I want, slush socks. But the last time I saw you, you were black. You've turned red."

"Changed my mind."

The other mice arrived.

"Who are these two?" asked Mephitis.

"Some new friends," said Junior, grinning. "Pine, Laurel, this is my best friend, Mephitis. This is my Uncle Ereth."

The two mice gazed up at Ereth with wide eyes. "Is he a . . . porcupine?"

"Yeah."

"Then how come he's your uncle?"

"Come on," said Junior. "Anyone can be an uncle."

"Why are these two mice red?" demanded Ereth.

"They want to look like me," explained Junior, with a glance at Mephitis. The skunk grinned.

"Is that true?" snapped Ereth.

"Yes, sir," said Laurel.

"Galloping galingales!" cried Ereth. "Why?"

"It's doing the stinky red, sir," said Pine.

"We want to be just like Junior," added Laurel.

"Brainless butter buckets," muttered Ereth with a shake of his head. "The whole world has turned stupid. Where's your triangulated toothbrush of a mother?" he asked Junior. "Is she all right?"

"Sure," said Junior. "Except, listen to this." He told Ereth and Mephitis about the bulldozer as well as the man who had come from the deconstruction company.

"Messing around with people is tricky," said Ereth. "I

better look at this bulldozer. Show me where it is," he demanded.

"Oh, yes, sir," said Pine. "Be happy to. It's just over this way."

As Ereth, Pine, and Laurel went ahead, Junior turned to Mephitis. "Hey, how come the porcupine showed up?" he whispered.

Mephitis shrugged. "He's worried about your mother."

"He's always worried. Was he screaming at you?"

"Naw. We've been talking. Actually, he's pretty cool."

"He is?" said Junior.

"And he swears," said Mephitis, "a whole lot better than we do."

Up ahead, Pine said to Ereth, "You really don't have to worry about the bulldozer, sir. Miss Poppy will take care of everything."

"Maybe," muttered Ereth.

"And after she does, she's going to stay at Gray House and be the next leader of the whole family."

Ereth stopped short. "Frozen eyeball fungus," he cried. "She's not doing anything of the kind!"

"Oh, but she is, sir," said Laurel, shrinking back before the force of Ereth's anger.

"Who told you that?" cried Ereth.

"Her father, sir. Lungwort."

"Who the crispy toad gas does he think he is, telling Poppy what she can or can't do? He'll have to deal with me first. She is not going to stay here. Not if I have to knock down Gray House myself!"

CHAPTER 29

Poppy Tries to Plan

POPPY PLODDED SLOWLY BACK to Gray House. The bulldozer was a monster. A gigantic monster. And it would be driven by unapproachable humans. It was simply unstoppable.

It didn't lift Poppy's spirits that as she walked among the mice, more than one called, "Hey, Poppy, have you figured out what we're going to do yet?" Or, "Just tell us what to do, Poppy. We'll do it!" Or, "Come up with something quick, Poppy! That thing is coming soon!"

When she climbed the steps into Gray House, Sweet Cicely was waiting. "Oh, Poppy, you've made your father so happy."

Poppy blinked. "Have I?"

"Naming your son 'Lungwort.' It made Papa feel so good. You were just teasing me about having named him Ragweed, weren't you?"

"Well, Mama, actually—"

"I am so gullible, I know," said Sweet Cicely with a giggle. "But if I can make you all laugh, particularly in times like these, I suppose it's perfectly fine." She brushed her ears nervously.

"Mama, I don't think—"

"Poppy!"

Poppy stopped mid-sentence and turned. Lilly was vigorously shaking her head.

"I think it was nice of you to name your youngster after Papa, too," said Lilly, gazing sternly at her sister. She drew Poppy away from Sweet Cicely.

"But Lilly," Poppy protested, "you know—"

"Never mind," said Lilly. "Papa wants to speak to you."

"Lilly," Poppy insisted as they went toward the old boot, "Junior's name is Ragweed."

"I don't know who told Papa his name was Lungwort, but it was a clever thing to do."

"Junior told him," said Poppy.

"Then he's a lot smarter than I thought."

Poppy stopped walking.

"Poppy, Papa is waiting for you."

"He can wait a moment longer."

"You sound just like Junior."

"Lilly, I have no idea what to do about the bulldozer."

"You really don't?"

Poppy shook her head. "Instead of worrying about me, what you should be doing is putting *your* mind to it," she said as she stepped behind the plaid curtain into the boot.

"Is that you, Poppy?" called Lungwort as she hurried down to the dim toe.

"Yes, Papa."

"Did you bring young Lungwort?"

"No, Papa."

"That's a fine young mouse you have there. Very fine. As for his painting himself red—and that smell—that's only youthful foolishness. My advice is to pay it no mind. The truth is, he reminds me of some of the things I did when I was his age."

"So he said. Things I never heard about."

Lungwort coughed. "It's grandparents, not parents, who are allowed to tell the truth. But never mind all that. Have you worked out a plan about the bulldozer?"

"No, Papa."

The old mouse leaned toward his daughter and lowered his voice. "Poppy, you don't seem to understand: it's urgent."

"Papa, I can't think of anything."

"But that's why I sent for you!"

"Then I suggest you make a plan for when they *do* knock the house down. Move to New House. At least everyone would be safe."

"Never. I won't accept such an outcome," cried Lungwort. "Since Gray House must remain, I will remain with it! As for being safe somewhere else, a captain goes down with his ship. If the house goes down, I intend to go down with it!"

"Papa!"

"Poppy! Do you wish to be responsible for my death?"

"That's ridiculous," said Poppy, and she turned to go.

"There's one more thing," Lungwort called.

"Yes, Papa," said a tired Poppy.

"Your son told me that you've become friends with a porcupine."

"His name is Ereth. He's a wonderful friend."

"That speaks poorly of you. I didn't raise you up to like porcupines. They are not to be trusted. They are destructive creatures. They eat mice."

"Nonsense. Porcupines do not eat mice, or any other creature. Ereth eats tree bark and, if he can find it, salt. And, Papa, Ereth wouldn't hurt a fly."

"It's you who are mistaken," insisted Lungwort. "Don't you dare bring him here."

"I wish I could. Unfortunately I already told him not to come."

"I shall hold you to that," said Lungwort, collapsing into a coughing fit. "Tell Lilly I'm out of pine seeds."

Poppy, unable to think of anything more to say, left the boot. *It's time to go home*, she decided.

CHAPTER 30

An E-mail

To: Bulldriver@Text.com

Subject: Old Lamout Farmhouse

Thanks for your report about the old Lamout place.
Sounds like an easy job. I suggest you go right back and
knock it down. Today. Just make sure you crush it all
into small enough bits so it can be hauled away easily.

Thanks,

Derrida Deconstruction Co.

CHAPTER 31

The Bulldozer

It's so big!" said Mephitis, his bushy tail twitching as he stared up at the towering bulldozer. He was standing between Ereth and Junior. With them were Laurel and Pine, who were also gazing up at the machine.

"Horsefly hockey," muttered Ereth. "Trees are a lot bigger."

"Yeah, right," said Junior. "Only trees stay put. This monster moves. I saw it. It was wicked scary."

Mephitis looked over his shoulder at Gray House. "Is it really going to knock the house down?"

"Everyone says so," said Pine.

"I wish they would just find a new house," added Laurel. "It's so crowded here. No one likes it."

"Long as Poppy gets back to the snag," muttered Ereth, "I don't care."

"Come on, Uncle Ereth," said Junior. "What are you so worried about? No way is Mama going to stay here."

"Lungwort said she would," said Laurel.

"Lungwort is just a potted pilgarlic," said Ereth.

Pine started to laugh.

"He does talk a lot," agreed Laurel.

"Maybe," said Ereth, "I need to go and give him a piece of my tail."

"Maybe," said Junior, still staring up at the bulldozer, "we need to figure out this thing first."

"I could lay down some stink all over it," said Mephitis. "Think that might help?"

"It would be better," said Pine, "if you gave *us* some stink."

"Yeah," agreed Laurel. "That's what we need."

"Livid crab licorice," said Ereth, looking around at the two mice. "Do you really want that smell?"

"Then we'd be just like Junior," said Pine.

"Doing the stinky red," Laurel explained.

Junior belched his approval.

"Wow! You are so amazing," said Laurel. "I hope you teach us that, too."

"You really want my stink?" the skunk asked the mice.

"Sure do!" the mice chorused.

"Stand over there," said Mephitis.

"I don't want any part of this," muttered Ereth. He stood up on his hind legs, grabbed hold of the bulldozer treads, and pulled himself up. At the same time the two mice ran off a few paces and, with their backs toward Mephitis, called, "Ready!"

"Keep your eyes closed!" the skunk ordered. When they did, he turned, stood up on his forepaws, aimed his backside at the mice, and blew out a cloud of stink that settled over them.

Giggling, the two mice rubbed themselves all over. Then Laurel sniffed Pine even as Pine sniffed Laurel. "That's wicked wild!" cried Pine.

"Yes," cried Laurel. "The stinky red!"

"Yo, dude," cried a laughing Junior. "Now you're just like me. All you have to do is learn to belch."

"Later," said Laurel. "Come on," she said to Pine. "I know some of my cousins who'll want to do the stinky red, too!"

The two mice ran off.

Junior climbed up onto the bulldozer. "Hey," he called to Mephitis, "come on up here. Maybe we can find a way to take this thing apart."

"I think you should leave it alone," said Ereth as the skunk crawled up the bulldozer to join them.

"Just saying we should try and fix it so it won't move," said Junior.

"I told you," said the porcupine, "I *want* them to knock the house down."

"Uncle Ereth, that's so dumb!" said Junior. "If they knock the house down, Ma's whole family will move into Dimwood Forest! You want Aunt Lilly for a neighbor?"

"Barking doggerols," cried Ereth. "I never thought of that! All right, let's take this thing apart!" He scampered into the cab.

All three sniffed about, trying to make sense of the pedals and levers.

"Too much metal," announced Ereth. "There's nothing to chew."

"Hey," said Junior, "what's all this stuff?" Reaching up, he grasped a lever and tried to pull it. He wasn't big or strong enough to make it budge.

Ereth continued to search and sniff about. Suddenly he sat up. "Salt," he cried out. "I smell salt!" Beginning to drool, the porcupine hastily hauled himself up to the driver's seat. He inhaled deeply, leaned out, and put his nose to a handle. "Chipped caterpillar custard! There's salt here," he announced, and started to lick it.

"How did it get there?" Junior asked.

"Human sweat," Ereth managed to say between slobbers. "It's the only good thing about them."

Mephitis, meanwhile, caught sight of the dangling chain that was attached to the engine key. He pulled at it, but it didn't move.

"Hey! Let me help you," called Junior. He grabbed hold of the chain and hauled himself up, kicking his rear legs as he went. Once he got to the key, he tried to pull it out. It would not move.

"Try twisting it," suggested Mephitis.

Junior reached around the key with his forepaws and hugged it, flattening his whole body to it. Then he kicked

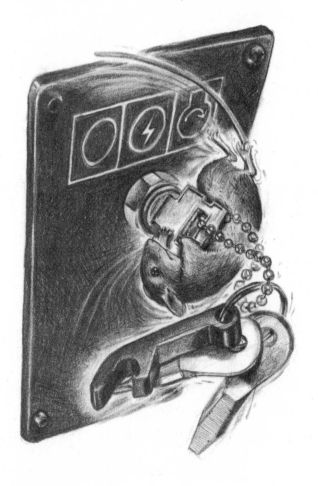

up again while waving his tail. He kicked so hard that the key levered up and around, flipping Junior, which caused him to loosen his grip and drop.

With a roar, the motor began to churn.

Ereth, startled by the noise, fell hard against the lever he had been licking, shoving it forward. Next moment the bulldozer began to move.

"Hey!" cried Junior from the floor of the cab. "What's happening?"

Ereth, righting himself, looked around. "Sugared squash rackets! This thing is moving!"

"How did that happen?" said Mephitis, trying to hold on.

Junior righted himself, then climbed up to the driver's seat and then up to the dashboard. "Uncle Ereth," he shouted, "you better do something!"

"Why should I do something, fuzz ball? You started the motor, not me!"

"But I don't know what to do!"

"How did you start it?"

"It must have been the key. I think I turned it."

"Then turn it back, banana brain. Turn it back!"

"Whoa," called Mephitis, "this thing moves fast."

Junior leaped for the key, grabbed it, clung to it with his whole body, and tried to twist it around. It was no use.

"Pancake puddles!" screamed Ereth. "Turn it off!"

"I can't!" Junior shouted.

Mephitis hauled himself up to the seat, sat up, and looked out. "Hey, guess what?" he said.

"What?"

"We're heading right for Gray House."

CHAPTER 32

The Bulldozer Comes

The bulldozer is coming! The bulldozer is coming!"

Poppy was chatting with Basil on the back steps when the frightful cry rang out.

The two mice leaped up and ran through the house to the front porch. Frightened mice were racing in all directions, squealing, squeaking, crying, screaming, and yelling. As they tried to reach safety, they pushed and shoved one another. Some leaped headlong off the porch. The mice in the yard raced away as fast as they could go into tall grass.

Poppy looked beyond the milling mice. Sure enough, the gigantic yellow bulldozer was moving slowly but relentlessly toward the house. "Basil," she shouted over the din, "I need to get Lungwort out!"

"I need to get to my wife and kids," said Basil, and raced off.

Bucking the flow of the panicky crowd, Poppy plunged back into the house and hurried into the old boot. Lilly and Sweet Cicely were already there, trying to get the old mouse up out of his bed.

"What's happening?" demanded a coughing Lungwort as he reached for his thimble cap and tried to put it on his head. He managed, though it perched in lopsided fashion. "Where is Poppy?" he demanded.

"I'm right here, Papa," cried Poppy. "You need to get out of the house right away. The bulldozer is coming."

"Coming? When? Where?"

"This very second! It's about to knock the house down."

"How close is it?" Lilly asked.

"It'll be here in minutes. The house is sure to collapse."

"Oh dear," cried Sweet Cicely. "Why must this happen right in the middle of Lungwort's nap?"

Lungwort managed to get up but pulled himself free from Sweet Cicely's grasp. "Let me go, drat it! I can move on my own."

"Dearest," implored Sweet Cicely, taking hold of Lungwort again. "You really must leave the house."

"Never!" cried Lungwort. "A mouse goes down with his house. Poppy, why aren't you doing something?"

"Papa," cried Lilly. "If you stay, you're going to be killed."

"Who would be mad enough to destroy Gray House?" cried Lungwort.

"What does it matter, Papa?" said Lilly. "It's happening."

Lungwort blinked, as if finally understanding. "But . . . but then what should I do?" he cried.

"Papa," said Poppy. "Listen to Lilly! She knows best."

Lungwort looked around. "She does?"

"Yes!"

With Lungwort allowing himself to be helped, they all began to move out of the boot.

"But who is committing this heinous crime?" the old mouse demanded as they approached the front door of the house. "What terrible beast is doing this? I demand an answer!"

"Please, Papa," said Lilly. "There's no time to talk. We just need to get out of the house."

"But what will happen to us?" said Lungwort. "This is the only home we have!"

"You can decide later," said Lilly. "Your safety is what's important now."

On the porch most of the mice had already fled to secure locations at some distance from the house. Poppy could see them scattered through the grass, staring with a mix of horror and fascination at the huge bulldozer, which was still moving, though at a painfully slow pace, toward

the house. The horrifying vision was made even worse by the spewing of black fumes and the deafening snarl of the motor.

"This way, dearest," Sweet Cicely coaxed as she and Lilly urged, pushed, and pulled Lungwort down the porch steps.

Poppy, keeping a vigilant eye on the approaching bulldozer, came right behind. Suddenly she realized she was not seeing a human in the cab. She was so baffled she stopped and stared: the bulldozer appeared to be moving entirely on its own.

Lungwort, supported by Sweet Cicely and led by Lilly, reached the ground and moved haltingly to safety. As Poppy followed, she stole a look back. No one was coming out the door. It appeared as if the entire house had been evacuated.

She turned back to the bulldozer. The great machine was rumbling forward, drawing ever closer to Gray House. As Poppy fixed her eyes on it, she knew with wrenching certainty there was no way it could avoid striking the house. The structure was doomed. Even so, she did not move. Why, she kept asking herself, was no one driving the machine?

As the bulldozer drew ever nearer, Poppy told herself she absolutely must move. She was just about to leap for safety when she suddenly saw a head pop up in the bulldozer cab. It was Ereth.

Poppy opened her mouth in astonishment. The next moment she saw Mephitis lift his head. And there, standing atop the cab's dashboard was Junior, his red fur a sharp contrast to the bulldozer's dirty yellow color.

There being no time to stand there flabbergasted, Poppy raced to the end of the porch and dived onto the grass below. Landing awkwardly, she picked herself up, gave herself a shake, ran a few feet, then turned to look back.

Every eye of every mouse was fixed upon the bulldozer.

The machine struck Gray House, its great blade smacking the structure squarely with a horrendous crunching sound. The porch collapsed. The front wall of the house caved in. Glass windows shattered in a storm of tinkling—like wind chimes gone mad. The attic floor dropped. The roof buckled. Cedar shingles popped, flying in every direction as if they were wet watermelon seeds. A cracking and snapping filled the air, like a fusillade of

firecrackers. And over it all a great plume of dust bloomed in the shape of a blossoming flower.

Even then the bulldozer did not stop. With a shudder and shake and an increased roar of its engine, its exhaust tailpipe billowing black smoke, it pushed on. For just a moment it seemed to strain, trembling—until, with an appalling, ear-blasting crack, the old house—or the heap that it had become—snapped off its foundation. That achieved, the bulldozer gathered new momentum and plowed on. The mountainous mass of misshapen house,

which now looked more like a gigantic overturned bird's
nest, began to slide along the ground, the entire pile heading for the Old Orchard.

The mice, standing in what was once the front yard of
the house, watched in awestruck silence.

The bulldozer was anything but quiet. Roaring, spewing
ghastly fumes, it shoved the mangled wreckage until the
great heap went hard up against an old apple tree. There
the machine churned and stopped its forward movement.
With a final barking burst of noxious fumes, the engine

sputtered, gave a terrible shudder, and produced an enormous belch before at last falling into a profound hush.

In the absolute silence that followed, nothing—no mouse, no bird, no leaf—dared move.

Poppy, having witnessed the entire event, could think of nothing but whether anyone else had noticed what she had: that Ereth, Junior, and Mephitis were in the driver's cab.

The answer came quickly. Into the deep and painful silence came Lungwort's bellowing, hacking voice: "That machine was driven by a porcupine!"

Poppy ran for the bulldozer.

CHAPTER 33

Introductions

W HEN THE BULLDOZER FINALLY CAME to a stop, Ereth gave a woozy shake of his head. "I don't know what to say," he muttered. Junior, Mephitis, and he stared out from the cab. The broken bits that had once been Gray House lay in a colossal heap before them. From it a curl of dust rose like a twist of frayed ribbon.

"Wow," muttered Junior, "that was freaking nasty."

"Awesome," agreed Mephitis, trying not to look at Junior. "Did you hear that machine belch?"

"Ultimate wicked!" said Junior, but he quickly turned to Ereth.

"Uncle Ereth?" he said.

Ereth shook his head. "What?"

"Please don't tell my mama."

Junior and Mephitis finally looked at each other. When they did, they started to laugh—and could not stop. Mephitis laughed so hard, he fell down, rolled over, stuck his stumpy legs into the air and churned them as if he were galloping. Junior, shrieking "Was that bad, or was that really bad," leaned his head against the cab well, held his stomach with one front paw, and wiped away tears with the other. Then he reached toward the skunk and cried, "Dude, that was the baddest doings in the whole wide universe!"

Mephitis slapped Junior's paw with a resounding smack. He was so excited he jumped onto the engine cowling, turned upside down on his front paws, and sent a cloud of stink over the bulldozer!

"Frosting on the cake!" shrieked Junior. "Frosting on the cake!" He was shaking so hard with laughter, he fell down backward.

"No one is going to believe this!" said Mephitis as he crawled back into the cab. "No one!" He and his buddy slapped paws anew.

"Stop that!" screamed Ereth. "Don't you realize what's happened?"

"We've . . . blown . . . the house . . . down!" sputtered Junior through his laughter.

"Demolished it—completely," said Mephitis, struggling to keep from laughing and failing. "I mean there's . . . nothing left."

"Nothing!" cried Junior.

"Let's just hope no one was inside," said Ereth.

"Oh my gosh," said Junior, laughing no more. "Do you think there might be?"

"Could be."

"But . . . that would be awful," said an equally sober Mephitis.

Next moment a voice called to them from below. "Ereth! Junior! Mephitis! What have you done with this horrid machine?"

They looked down. It was Poppy. She was standing by the bulldozer's side and looking up.

"Done?" said Ereth. "What do you think, fly fidget: I was trying to stop it."

"Trying to stop it?" cried Poppy. "Do you understand what you've done?"

"Me?" said Ereth. "What makes you think it had anything to do with me?"

"You are the responsible adult."

"I am?"

"Of course you are!"

Ereth looked at Junior. Junior looked at him. The young mouse was clenching his teeth tightly to keep from breaking into laughter again. Mephitis turned away.

"Ereth," cried Poppy. "Can't you see that you've completely destroyed Gray House!"

"Hey, Mama," Junior managed to say. "I thought it was going to happen anyway."

"But not by you," cried Poppy. "Erethizon Dorsatum, why are you even here?"

"Guess why, fudge whiskers. To protect you."

To keep from laughing, Junior had to stuff a paw into his mouth.

Exasperated to the point of speechlessness, Poppy turned away and scanned the wreckage. Atop the pile she spied her old Log Cabin Syrup can, badly dented.

"Unbelievable," she whispered, as much to herself as anyone. "Unbelievable."

"Miss Poppy . . . ," muttered Mephitis.

"What?"

"I'm sorry."

"Sorry?" Poppy managed to say.

"Come on, Mama," said Junior, coming to his friend's defense. "You said you wanted to be cool, didn't you? You don't think we *meant* to do it, do you?"

By this time the other mice, still in shock but sensing that the danger from the machine had passed, had begun to gather around both the wreckage and the bulldozer. They stared at it in silence.

"That's a ridiculous, irresponsible response," said Poppy, gazing at the wreckage. "A disaster. Totally . . . one hundred percent unacceptable!" She wrinkled her nose. "And what's that stench?" she demanded.

"Mephitis got a little excited," said Junior, giggling.

"Excited!"

"Sorry," muttered Mephitis a second time, while making sure he did not look at Junior.

"How did you even get this machine to move?" Poppy demanded.

"Uncle Ereth," said Junior, "fell onto a lever just as I

was turning the key. It began to move. On its own."

"Ereth," said Poppy, "is that true? Are you the one to blame for this?"

"Actually," muttered Ereth in such a low voice that Poppy was not certain she heard right, "actually, it was the salt's fault."

CHAPTER 34

The Wreckage

CONFIDENT THAT AT LAST the bulldozer had truly halted, some of the mice began to approach the wreckage of the house, poking and prodding it. Others continued to stare at the bulldozer. A few gazed nervously up at Ereth and Mephitis.

Last to arrive was the slow-moving Lungwort, still supported by Lilly and Sweet Cicely.

"There!" cried the old mouse as he came through the crowd of onlookers. "Didn't I tell you porcupines were the most dangerous creatures on earth?"

"Who's that?" Ereth demanded of Poppy, lifting his head.

Poppy sighed. "It's my father, Lungwort. Papa, I'd like you to meet Ereth, my friend."

"Friend!" sputtered Lungwort. "This so-called friend of yours was driving that machine! He's the one responsible for smashing down our dearly loved house."

Poppy took a deep breath, offered a reproachful look

at Ereth, and said, "I'm afraid so."

"Grandpa," said Junior.

"What?"

"It wasn't Ereth. It was me. I did it."

"Impossible. How could you?"

"I turned the key. Really. It was my fault."

"Please," said Poppy, "all three of you, come down here. I'm afraid we need to make some introductions—and explanations."

Ereth, Mephitis, and Junior reluctantly climbed down from the bulldozer. The mice gathered around, staring. Mephitis and Junior, side by side, kept bumping each other, suppressing giggles. An embarrassed Ereth scowled, his tail twitching.

"Ereth, I should like you to meet my parents," began Poppy. "Papa, Mama, this is Ereth. This is Junior's friend Mephitis."

"Keep that porcupine away from me!" cried Lungwort, backing away. "Porcupines are a menace. A danger. A threat to the peace. And he stinks. Away with him!"

"Cardboard crocodiles," Ereth said, turning to Poppy with a look of exasperation.

"Uncle Ereth," said Junior, "I don't think he likes you."

"Well, I don't like him, either! He's just a toilet bowl of nose drip!"

"And who are you," shouted an enraged Lungwort. "You . . . you bumbling beast of destruction!"

"See here, you—," Ereth began to reply.

"Ereth," shouted Poppy with all her breath. "For once, be quiet!"

"Mice cavorting with porcupines and skunks," cried Lungwort. "The world's gone insane. I want nothing to do with it! Poppy, if this is the way you would lead the family, I clearly have made a grave mistake. Is there no one who understands me?" he cried.

Lilly held out a paw. "Papa, would you like a pine seed?"

Lungwort stared at her and blinked. "Lilly," he cried, "it's perfectly clear you should be the head of the family!"

With a snort, Lungwort pulled off his thimble cap and brought it down on Lilly's head. Then, muttering under his breath, he marched haltingly away, Sweet Cicely and Lilly by his side. Lilly, reaching up to touch the cap, tried to suppress a smile—but could not.

Even as she did, a mouse in the yard called out, "Look! A human just arrived!"

All the animals turned their attention to Tar Road. Sure enough, a pickup truck had driven up and stopped. The next moment a man stepped out.

CHAPTER 35

A Discovery

THE MAN WHO GOT OUT of the truck was the same one—tan overalls and large stomach—who had come before. Now he stood by the side of the truck and looked about where the bulldozer had been. Puzzled by what he was not seeing, he pulled at the peak of his cap a couple of times. Then he spied the collapsed house and the bulldozer. He stared, puzzlement deepening. With another tug on his cap, he moved cautiously toward the wreckage.

The mice scattered.

As for Ereth and Mephitis, they ran behind the wreckage and crouched down. Poppy and Junior were with them.

"I don't know how I am ever going to forgive you for this," Poppy whispered.

"Freckled pork feathers," said Ereth, "who are you talking to?"

"Each and every one of you!"

"But—"

"Ereth, for once, keep still!"

Junior belched. Mephitis giggled. Poppy looked at them severely.

Up by the road, the man moved slowly, as if unsure what he was seeing. A few times he paused and looked around. When he came to the place where Gray House had stood, he gazed at the shorn foundation.

After a moment he continued on toward the bulldozer and the wreck of the house. Drawing near, he considered the mess, then suddenly turned away, covering his nose with his hands.

A grinning Junior turned to Mephitis and whispered, "You got him, dude!"

"Shhh!" said Poppy.

The man, one hand holding his nose, climbed into the bulldozer and turned the key. There was a grinding, clacking noise, but the motor did not start. Baffled, the man pocketed the key and hurried back toward his truck, looking over his shoulder, once, then twice, his brow deeply furrowed.

"Where's he going?" asked Junior as they stepped out from their hiding place to watch him.

"Let's hope it's to his own home," said Poppy.

Just as the man approached his truck, Laurel and Pine, with a troop of their young friends, appeared. Every one

of them had red fur. Unaware of what had happened at
Gray House, they had gone to where the bulldozer had
been.

Arriving at his truck, the man turned to take one last
look back. As he saw the red mice, he halted and gasped.
When the mice began to belch, he jumped into the truck
and raced away.

It was Junior who said, "Cool, I think those red mice
scared him."

"Hey, everyone!"

The mice all turned. Atop the pile of rubble stood Basil. "This place has a million rooms now!" he cried. "Everyone can have a little space and privacy!"

There was a general squeal of delight as all the mice raced for the wreck and began to explore.

CHAPTER 36

Farewells

A FEW HOURS LATER, deep within the mass of rubble that had once been Gray House, in the space Lilly had found for Lungwort and Sweet Cicely, Poppy and Junior said their farewells. Lilly, the thimble cap on her head, was there, too.

"I need to say good-bye, Papa," said Poppy.

"Humph," muttered Lungwort.

"Papa," said Lilly, "it's really worked out well. There's room, private room, for everyone. It's so much better for the family. We can stay together without being on top of one another."

"Porcupines," Lungwort said under his breath. *"Porcupines!"*

Sweet Cicely gave a hug to Junior and then one to Poppy. "It was good to see you," she said. "Do you think you might come again . . . soon?"

Poppy, wondering whether it was a question or a warning, simply said, "We'll see."

Lilly walked them out beyond the wreckage.

"Poppy," she said, "thank you."

"For what?"

"Being you."

They exchanged another hug. This time they meant it.

CHAPTER 37

Heading Home

POPPY, ERETH, JUNIOR, AND MEPHITIS were moving along an animal trail deep in Dimwood Forest. They were going home.

"Scat stew with sandpaper," said Ereth to Poppy. "How could you have a father like that?"

"Very few creatures get to choose their fathers," Poppy reminded him.

"Or mothers," added Junior, with a belch.

"You're lucky anyone chose you," returned Poppy. "Just remember, you all destroyed that house."

"Oh, purple pretzel puppies," said the porcupine. "It was just a mistake."

"*Just?*"

"Miss Poppy," said Mephitis. "Really. We didn't mean it."

"I'm sure," said Poppy with a sigh.

"Anyway, it turned out okay," said Junior. "They all

found their own places. You heard them: they like it better this way."

"I suppose a little privacy among families is a good thing," agreed Poppy.

Suddenly Ereth stopped. "That reminds me," he said, "I have to go somewhere."

"Where?"

"To find some peace and quiet, bilge brain. If that's all right with you?"

"Ereth, as always, you may do whatever you like."

"Right," muttered the old porcupine. He turned to Mephitis. "You coming, Misfit?"

"Coming where?" cried an alarmed Junior.

Mephitis looked about shyly. "Ereth said I could live with him in his log."

"He did?" said Poppy, looking first at the skunk and then at the porcupine.

"But I'm not cleaning up after him," said Ereth, "or feeding him, or teaching him, or taking care of him, or talking to him in any way whatsoever unless *I* want to. And the first time he stinks up the place or belches or says 'freaking,' he's out. Gone. Done! Kaput!"

"But then," asked Poppy, trying not to smile too broadly, "what *are* you going to do with him?"

Mephitis looked to Ereth. "Tell her yourself, Stink Star," said the porcupine.

"He's . . . going to teach me to swear," said Mephitis.

Poppy ran over to Ereth, stood on her hind legs, and kissed him on the tip of his nose. Then she ran over to Mephitis and did the same. "Welcome to our neighborhood," she said.

"French-fried Foos balls," Ereth muttered. With crossed eyes focused on the tip of his nose, he plunged into the woods and was quickly lost to view. Mephitis hesitated, looked at Junior, grinned, and said, "See you later, pal." Then he trundled after Ereth as fast as his own short legs would take him.

"Cool," said Junior. "That means he'll be living right next to us."

As Poppy and Junior resumed their walk, she said, "Junior, I do have to ask you something: you've never said what you think of my parents."

"Oh yeah. Well, your mother is a wilted flower. Your father is funny—but I don't think he means to be."

"No . . . what I mean, is, do you think . . . I'm . . . like them?"

"Do you want to be?"

"I don't think so."

"Well, you aren't," said Junior. "No more than I want to be like you or Papa. But I'd like to go back."

Poppy stopped. "You would?"

"Yeah. See, there was this mouse, name of Laurel. . . ."

Poppy gazed at Junior. "What about her?"

"Oh, I don't know," said Junior, looking everywhere but at Poppy. "Sort of wicked."

Poppy was sure his red fur turned a shade redder.

"What's with you?" Junior asked, finally getting the courage to look at his mother.

"Ragweed Junior, have I told you recently how much I love you?"

Junior laughed. "Hey, a mouse has to do what a mouse has to do."

"Well, I do love you!" she cried as she gave him a hug. After a moment he returned it.

CHAPTER 38

Another E-mail

To: DerridaDeconstructionCompany.com
Subject: Old Lamout Farmhouse

Went out to the old Lamout place. Bulldozer had been
moved. House crushed. Mice, smelling like skunks,
have turned red. They belch a lot, too. Something really
weird going on there. I'd suggest you stay away—as
long as there are red mice, anyway.

CHAPTER 39

Poppy's Return

It was late afternoon when Poppy and Junior reached the snag. Mariposa, Verbena, and Crabgrass were playing out front. Mariposa saw Poppy first. "It's Mama! And Junior!" she cried.

In moments the rest of the family poured out of the snag and clung to Poppy, trying to pull her in as many directions as possible. Rye was there, too, standing back but grinning broadly.

"How did it go?" he called over the squeaky din.

"It was a smash!" said Junior.

Not until late that night did Poppy and Rye find a moment to be alone. It was then she told him all that had happened.

Then he asked, "Was it worth the going?"

"I suppose. But do you know the best thing about going away?" said Poppy.

"What's that?"

"Coming home," said Poppy. "To all of you. 'Specially you." She took up Rye's paw and held it.

Side by side, Poppy and Rye watched as a thin crescent moon, high in the sky, shed faint light over Dimwood Forest. The chirp of crickets counted the quiet moments.

"Rye?" said Poppy after a while.

"What?"

"I think I'm getting old."

Rye leaned over, gave her a nuzzle, and into her ear whispered, "You're just changing—again."